GW00499203

Dedication

For my mum, (Christine Jolliff),
Because of her continued support throughout my life. She's
helped me in more ways than anyone else.

In loving memory of my dad, (David Jolliff), for buying us the
ponies, horses and taking us to shows.

And to Natalie, you are always my sister and forever my friend.

Acknowledgements

I would like to thank my husband, Steve, and son, Milo, for putting up with me having my head in my laptop for hours. Deborah Carr for answering all my writing questions; there has been loads.

For all of my sisters and friends for the research feedback:-

Natalie Smith
James Watson
Rachel Roffe
Paul Brock
Olly Franklin
Royston Prisk
David Gebbels
Jean Day
Kate Foster
Craig Barlow
Teressa Pickford
Emma-Jane Rose
Helen Easty
Em Nicholls
Robert Wilmot
James Davies
Cheryl Baxendale
Fiona Prentice
David Sullivan
Kate Hirons Mather
Ben Clargo
James Liddell
Kate Moulson
Edward 'Shovel Hands' Mills
Jason Gudge
Christie Wallis

Bob Maclintock
Pat Winman
Tina Hall
Tracey Hawkins
Howard Smith
Brian Gummer

Thank you to Amanda Anderson for beta reading for me.
Keith & Yvette Walter for being such wonderful one in a million
friends over the miles.

For the bale push:-

Haydn Williams
Olly Franklin
Russell Deeley
Neil Lambert
Dibber Franklin
Mark Bowerman
Charles 'Bimmer' Franklin
Lesley McDermott
Emma-Jane Rose
Brian Butler
Keith Butler
Peter Butler
Claire Butler
Rob Bustin
Kelly Sargent
Paul Stork
Lee Walker
Martin Franklin
Alan Gaskins
Colin Haynes
Roy Haynes

To Karen Bassett for giving me my sanity back.

For their constant friendship and support over the years
Peter Hill
Elizabeth Bowness
Brian Gummer

CHAPTER 1

It was 1973 and twins were born to Walter and Yvette Keith. They were identical twins, born just four minutes apart. The twins were girls, named Gabriella (Gabby for short) and Florence. They lived in a small town called Wrenbridge. The Keith family were very close. Yvette was a stay-at-home mum and Walter worked hard on his rapidly expanding business to ensure they all had a comfortable life. He was a popular businessman working in the paper industry and there was a lot of money to be made by recycling paper.

The four of them lived in a three-bedroom house in Wrenbridge.

The house was always full of noise as the girls had lots of animals and music was constant.

They had a cat called Tiddles and a beautiful dog called Bandit.

Both of these animals grew up with Gabby and Florence and they were part of the family.

They would all go out on long walks with Bandit and spend time walking across fields and on many occasions, they would end up with one of them losing a boot whilst walking through some particularly sticky mud. Which, needless to say, Walter had to retrieve.

Gabby and Florence were painfully shy growing up. On starting primary school, they were both so scared and shy that they both sat on one chair together. They had lots of friends at school but were still terribly shy to anyone new. Both girls worked hard during school. They were not allowed to sit next to each other during tests as they would get accused of cheating, after getting the same amount of questions right and wrong. They didn't understand the power of twins. They had a connection where they did the same things at the same time. And during school, this baffled the teachers.

Gabby and Florence went to a normal local primary school which was just a mile down the road. They would walk to school with their mum or she would drive them if it was raining. Gabby's mum and dad did a lot to help the school. When there were school fetes, Yvette would spend hours baking for the cake stand and Walter would go around helping to set up the stands. It was a small town and most parents knew each other from their own school days.

When they were seven, Gabby and Florence's parents asked 'How would you like to try horse-riding?' The girls were over the moon. Gabby could not wait and wanted to know exactly when they were going, what they needed to wear and do they know the name of the ponies they'd be riding? Questions that didn't get answered until they actually arrived at the riding school on the following Saturday.

The yard belonged to Margaret and George Knight. It was a small yard but they had a lot of horses that were mainly kept outside. They lead out two ponies when they arrived that Saturday. Florence was put on a bay-coloured pony called Dan and Gabby was put on a grey pony called Silver. They were lead around a small paddock and shown how to hold the reins and where to position their feet. They were also taught how to trot that day too. George lead Gabby around shouting out 'up, down, up, down' as they trotted along. Gabby was bumping around on the pony's back trying to make her ups, up and her downs, down.

After that lesson, the girls both totally fell in love with horses.

They both carried on riding at those stables each week for some years.

They loved it but after a while, they thought it was time to move on to a new riding school and learn more.

They ended up going to a new yard called North Moor Equestrian Centre and it was owned by Kelly Johns. Kelly was a well-respected horsewoman who had competed at high-level eventing so they knew this was someone they could learn a lot from.

Gabby and Florence soon discovered if they worked at weekends for the equestrian centre, there was a possibility of a free ride. So, each weekend, Gabby and Florence cycled up to the stables. They would take some lunch with them to keep them going and work at the equestrian centre, hoping to get a free ride at the end of the day. They would muck out the stables, tack up the horses and ponies ready for lessons, clean tack and lead beginners around. And all other duties that were given to them.

There were a lot of other girls there doing the same thing. All of them desperate for a ride. Kelly was good to them all and would let them ride the horses and ponies that hadn't been used that day or had only been out once. She would put up fun show jumping courses and get them all jumping or she'd make up games for them all. They had so much fun. Kelly was brilliant to the children who helped out. She knew that without them the equestrian centre wouldn't run as it did. They were valued and she was happy to make sure she let them all know how much she appreciated them being there.

CHAPTER 2

Gabby and Florence had a somewhat sheltered childhood. Walter was very strict and would be the one who dealt out the reprimands when needed. They were never physical but the girls were well aware of being taught to respect their elders and they didn't dare do anything they knew he wouldn't be happy about. Yvette, on the other hand, was loving and gentle and did everything in the house for them all. Nothing was too much trouble. She was always there when the girls got back from school and she always had Walter's dinner on the table when he came home from work.

Outside of school, the girls liked playing with the rest of the children on their road. They played games using elastic, did skipping together using an enormous long rope where they had one person each end and they would get the others to jump in and then out.

They also spent a lot of time riding their bikes. The girls would often sing a song together called Alice the Camel, where they would kick up their legs like they were doing a can-can dance.

Alice was also the name of the lady next door who would briskly come out and tell them all off, which they all found extremely funny. Whatever the weather they'd all be playing outside until being called back in for baths and bed.

When it was time to move to secondary school, Gabby and Florence went to Wrenbridge High School. This was the closest to where they lived and they would walk to school with friends. Each day, they would walk together and chat about who's done what the night before and talk about the lessons they would be having that day. During High School, Gabby was really bullied by a girl called Lorraine, who for some reason took a dislike to her and would do awful things to her every day. To start with, it was just words and she'd go home upset and tell her mum. Her mum would say 'It's just words, try to ignore it.' But then the physical stuff started happening. She was walking to Maths class one morning and they had three flights of stairs to walk up. Lorraine was ahead of her and leaned down and spat in Gabby's face. It was horrific. Gabby was so shocked and disgusted. But she didn't want to be late for her lesson so just wiped it off and carried on going. Things began to escalate after that. No amount of telling the teachers helped.

A few weeks later, she was walking to her English class and Lorraine pushed her over, she then grabbed Gabby's hair and dragged her down the corridor. This made loads of the other kids shout 'fight, fight, fight,' but nobody thought to help her.

Each day came a new cruel act. It was towards exam time and the girls were studying hard and were sat in a French lesson when Lorraine walked over to Gabby, punched her in the face and ran off. Gabby's nose started pouring with blood, it was going everywhere. All down her uniform, all over the floor, she rushed to the toilets but the bleeding wasn't stopping. Florence took her to see the school matron. She then spent the rest of her day with her head over a sink whilst her nose continued to bleed.

That afternoon when the bell went to go home, Gabby and Florence walked home. Gabby looked like she'd been involved in some kind of massacre as she was covered in blood. The sight of her walking in the house frightened the life out of Yvette when they walked in. Yvette got them some clean clothes out and scrubbed like mad at the blood stains.

That night when the girls were nearly ready for bed their year tutor arrived.

Gabby and Florence were worried about what he was going to say.

After what had happened that day, they were both really scared about going to school the next day. Walter let Mr Broom in and he spoke to them all about what had happened at school that day. He told them that Lorraine had a tough start in life and it was obviously fuelled by jealousy because Gabby and Florence had everything that she wanted. He said he knew that the police could charge her with assault but he didn't recommend them contacting them. He was reassuring them that this was something they had taken on board now and that they would be making sure nothing else happened, and they were going to be keeping a close eye on her.

Not feeling very reassured, Gabby went to bed that night with a feeling of dread for what was going to happen the next day. She had a restless sleep. Still, she got up and ready for school as normal.

Gabby was quiet on the way to school as she felt sick with worry. They walked as usual.

The route to school takes them past their grandparent's house and then just a few more yards away were the bollards stopping cars from entering the school grounds.

It was then that Gabby spotted Lorraine waiting for her; she had a big lump of wood. It was clear what the intention for it was. Gabby and Florence immediately turned and ran all the way back home.

Walter went into the school to complain about the continued bullying. It was acknowledged, the school tried to stop it but throughout their time at that school, it never ceased.

Whilst at school, the girls started to notice boys. Boyfriends were never allowed. Walter would say they needed to concentrate on their school work. So, to even mention a boy was something that never happened with their parents. Gabby and Florence would chat with each other about which boys they fancied in school.

Both girls loved music and would spend hours shut in their bedroom learning the songs off the radio or cassettes, listening, then stopping and starting the songs so they could write down the lyrics until they had them all. They would learn them off by heart and make up dance routines which they would teach their friends and would then do the dance routine to the class in school.

CHAPTER 3

During half-term and summer holidays, Yvette
and Walter would take the girls on holiday,
which usually meant going to Dorset, Wales or
the New Forest. On one particular holiday, they
were going camping. Everyone was so excited
and they all got in the car at some ridiculous
hour of the morning. They felt like they were
getting up in the middle of the night. The girls
always fell asleep for part of the journey and on
waking up they would be given biscuits and
they would have some coffee from a flask. They
were all squashed up in the car and drove for
four hours to Wales.

When they got there, they were all desperate to
get out of the car and stretch their legs. And also,
Bandit was happy to finally be allowed to jump
out the car, have a run around and a wee. Gabby
and Florence decided to have a look around,
there were fields and mountains as far as the eye
could see. Gabby wanted to see how many
animals she could see from where they were and
spotted mainly hundreds of sheep and a few
cows further away in fields. She also spotted lots
of birds of prey flying around.

Whilst walking, she was daydreaming and looking around and came across a very unusual feather. She picked it up and immediately ran over to ask Walter what the bird was that it came from. He was a font of knowledge for all those kinds of things and he told her it came from a Peregrine Falcon. He was very impressed that she found such a rare feather. Gabby was overjoyed that it was something she hadn't heard of and was now on the hunt to find something even more interesting.

In the afternoon, they were all super-hot and right by where they had parked the car, there was a lake in part of the mountain. It wasn't very wide but you couldn't see the bottom. Walter went in and swam about so the girls could come in too. They both went in and had a lovely cool dip in the water. After the long journey in the car, it was a welcome relief. Yvette didn't get in with them, she sat on the side and wiggled her toes in the water and was on Bandit duty. They didn't want him to get in the water in case he couldn't get out. It would have been very difficult for a dog to climb out of the lake they were in.

Gabby and Florence soon found the cool water was beginning to make them feel a bit too cool so decided to get out and dry.

Yvette took this as the time to get some food on the go whilst they all got into some dry clothes.

She got the camping stove out of the car and
started heating up some beans and taking out
the bread they had taken with them from home.
They were all so hungry by then.
They all sat silently munching away and the
warm food soon began to make them feel sleepy.
Gabby helped her mum clean up and put the
cutlery away. They decided to all have an early
night. Walter had put up the tent and the girls
went into the smaller sleeping bags and got
snuggled up for the night. Yvette and Walter
finished clearing up and locked the car. Walter
took Bandit out for a last walk and then they too
came into the tent and settled down. They had
no problem sleeping that night, despite the cold.
The next morning, they all woke up bright and
early. It was crisp out so they threw on warm
clothes and went outside as there were other
people tootling about, getting breakfast ready
and chatting happily amongst themselves.
Walter had already gone out with Bandit and by
the time the girls and Yvette were getting
breakfast ready, he came back down towards
their tent and sat down with them where they all
ate a hearty breakfast. Yvette had made them
scrambled egg and toasted the bread.
During breakfast, they all discussed what they
were going to be doing that day.

Each day they were there was the same routine whilst eating; discussing where they would be going that day, exploring little villages nearby, a town, and also a beach. The mountain was their base and they all spent hours walking and stopping for picnics along the way. It was a magical time and something that would stay with them forever. The air was fresh and clean and was definitely good for the soul.

CHAPTER 4

For years, Gabby and Florence would go on and on to their parents to buy them a pony. They would complain that this person and that person had one already. Eventually, their parents agreed to buy them a pony. They all knew that buying a pony was a whole new experience and something they should have got help with looking back. They tried many ponies before they found the one. He happened to be the thirteenth pony they looked at. It was a 12.2hh Welsh x Arab, 10-year-old gelding called Sparkle. The girls rode him and took him on the road where they decided he was the right one. Walter chatted to the owner to sort out the money and then it was agreed they would go the following week to pick him up.

That week dragged for the girls and they could hardly concentrate at school for excitement. Finally, the weekend arrived and Walter had loaned a horse trailer from a friend and they all went off to fetch Sparkle. Gabby and Florence had been to the saddlery with Yvette to buy some travel bandages they would need to put on him and protect him whilst travelling.

They were all red and on a grey pony made him look very smart indeed.

They let him settle in and he got a lot of attention from the people at the equestrian centre. He was a very striking little pony and full of spirit. The following day, Gabby and Florence got up early to the yard and tacked him up ready to go out to ride. They decided with it being their first time in the new environment they would go to the indoor school. Gabby got on and started walking around. Sparkle was very fizzy and full of himself. He went up the long side of the indoor school and on making their way across to come back, he bolted. Gabby sat up and tried slowing him down but he was having none of it. He stopped when he got to the door, thankfully it was closed.

That day, they realised Sparkle was not what you'd call a first pony and they were going to have to learn to ride him fast if they wanted to stay on, otherwise they'd either be on the floor or in the next county.

Sparkle had previously been a Prince Philip cup pony where they do pony club games. He thought everything was a race.

He literally had no brakes but he had the biggest heart.

As they had just the one pony to share between them, Gabby and Florence would go out with Sparkle on hacks, riding on the roads and across bridle paths and pretend they were on two ponies. One of the girls would ride to where they were going and then they would swap on the way back. The one that was riding would go in front and the one on foot would run behind. They would pretend they were on a pony too. For the drivers going past, it must have been a hilarious sight. They probably thought the girls had lost a pony or lost the plot.

Seeing how the girls were totally dedicated to Sparkle, Yvette and Walter told them they could have another pony. They went to see a pony that was called Trigger. He was a 14.2hh, flea-bitten grey, Connemara x Arab. This time, they had him on a week's trial to make sure he was right for them. On riding him, he was the total opposite of Sparkle. He was a well-mannered pony. He seemed really big when they rode him after being used to just riding Sparkle but he was a really comfortable ride. He had lovely paces and his canter was a dream, lovely big strides but so smooth. They took him over some jumps and he did not hesitate jumping straight over. Gabby was in heaven, she felt like she could do anything. He was a joy to ride. They bought Trigger after that week. He had a stable next to Sparkle and they got on really well together.

Sparkle and Trigger were the girls' whole world. They took them on lots of different hacks, riding around the countryside. They would take some food and drinks and the ponies would also drink out of the flask cup when they stopped. They took the ponies through bridleways so they could spend most of the ride off the road.

They got to a field gate and where they were about to go through was a field full of pigs. The pigs were very interested in them. They got the gate open but the ponies were a bit spooked by the pigs so Florence got off and shut the gate as fast as she could. Instead of standing around, they made the decision to run across the field to the gate to get out the other side as fast as possible. The pigs chased them.

Trigger was particularly frightened as the pigs were so close to his back end. He tried to kick out and as he did, he got caught on the wire fence. Part of it got stuck between his shoe and his hoof. They got out of the field and both girls got off and tried to get the wire out. There was no way they could carry on with the ride with this wire stuck. Trigger would be lame and who knows what damage it could have done.

They took him gently into the farmyard and the farmer was outside.

They told him what had happened and he said he'd help them get the wire out.

He was really helpful. They both held on to Trigger whilst the farmer removed the wire. Trigger wasn't happy being close to this man, he smelt just like the pigs and Trigger was not sure about him at all but he got the wire out and they were very lucky as no damage was done.

CHAPTER 5

At age thirteen, they joined the pony club which was where they learnt so much more about horses' well-being, riding and stable management. The instructors were strict and made sure all the children were aware that they were there to learn and not mess about. They would be sent back to their parents if they did misbehave.

They went on rallies most weekends which is what the pony club call the lessons. One rally at a nearby farm which belonged to a friend was close enough to ride to that day. They had to go across a big main road but Sparkle and Trigger were bomb proof on the road so they had no problems.

When they got to the farm, they met up with a huge group of people also there for the fun ride. This was the first fun ride they had been on. Gabby was on Trigger and Florence was on Sparkle. On seeing the other ponies, Trigger and Sparkle started getting really excited and bouncing around. They were told what was happening and the group got split in two with there being so many of them.

As they set off, Sparkle decided it was also the time to take off so Florence spent all her time turning circles to slow him down. Trigger was cantering on the spot. He kept snatching the reins out of Gabby's hands and dragging his head down. She was having a battle to keep his head up. This was not their best rally.

After the fun ride, they were told by the pony club that their ponies were too dangerous so the girls continued to go to the dismounted rallies and in the meantime ride them for fun and competitions. When they turned 15, Walter bought them both a horse each. They were both suitable for pony club so they could now go to the rallies with them.

The horses were both completely different. One was a Thoroughbred and the other was a Welsh Cob. They had decided on these two horses but between them, Gabby and Florence decided to get to know them more before deciding which one they wanted as their own. Gabby liked Cardock the Thoroughbred best. He was a gentleman, quiet and well-mannered. Florence was happy with Misty, who was the Welsh Cob; she was a cheeky fun ride and would jump anything.

One pony club rally where Gabby rode Misty and Florence had Cardock, they had to jump over fences with their reins in a knot and hands out to the sides like an aeroplane.

This was total trust of the horses and great for their balance. That day the girls chose which horse they wanted for their own. Gabby chose Misty and Florence was happy as she wanted Cardock.

CHAPTER 6

When Walter bought the horses, they had to be kept at a different yard to the ponies as there wasn't room for all four at the same place. This meant spending a few weeks, going backwards and forwards from one yard to the next. It wasn't ideal and eventually, they managed to move the ponies to the same yard too. The yard had amazing facilities and they rode after school and each weekend. The lady who ran the yard was a fantastic rider and she would give the girls lessons. They also got to learn a lot from watching her ride and going to see her compete, which she did regularly.

On summer days, they would go to the yard early in the morning. The horses would be outside and they walked down to the field to get them in. Cardock and Misty were very good coming in and so too was Trigger.

Sparkle was a little devil to catch. Gabby and Florence would go in the field and lay on the grass. The ponies would be so curious wondering what on earth they were doing and they would walk over to them where they would then be able to grab hold of Sparkle's headcollar.

One day, they actually spent two hours trying to catch him. They crawled along the ground on that day to get the little cheeky chap in. They did that a lot and Sparkle never cottoned on that this was all down to him.

CHAPTER 7

At school, Gabby was now in the fifth year and her year tutor told them all they had to do for a week's work experience. As she was fully intending on riding and working with horses, she chose to go to The Wrenbridge Hunt Stables. Florence went too. They would help out with the mucking out and then go out on exercise. They rode different horses each day, preparing the horses for hunting, cleaning tack and then going out with the second horses in the lorry. They would then come back to the yard with the horses that went out first and get them all cleaned up and comfortable and have that tack to clean. Later in the afternoon, they would have the second horses back. The second horses would need to be washed off and bedded down for the evening. The girls would then have more tack to clean and then time to feed before they finished the day at the yard. It was really hard work but they both loved every minute of it. It was also a really good experience for the future. Before leaving school, they had discussions with their year tutor asking them what they had in mind for a career.

Gabby would constantly say she wanted to work with horses and they constantly tried to put her off. She was in a one-on-one with Mr Broom and he said to her 'What if one day, you break your back, then what will you do?'

Just to keep the school tutor happy and plus, the college she wanted to go to didn't accept her until she was seventeen and a half, she stayed on in the sixth form and did a secretarial course. Something to fall back on.

The girls spent all their time when not in school at the stable yard with their horses. They knew their school friends were out and about with boys but horses were more important to them at the time. They would go to different shows with the ponies on weekends.

One weekend, they took them to a show at Wrenbridge Hunt Stables. This was an annual show, one side was for horses and the other was for the terrier show. That year, they dressed themselves and their ponies up as St Trinians, which were naughty school girls from a television show. The girls put skirts on the ponies, by opening grey kilts and tying them on with bailing twine. They had straw hats with holes cut out for the ears and also put ties on them. They got second place but they were happy with that.

The ponies were also the ones to take part when Gabby and Florence took part in raising money for Telethon; it was a big charity event raising money for lots of different charities. Yvette and Walter walked along with them carrying buckets. They collected money going through different villages and cars would stop and give them money. They dressed for the occasion in there hacking jackets and ties and made sure the ponies were spotless.

When they got to one of the villages, it was around lunch time so the pub was very busy. Gabby took Sparkle in the pub. He was not fazed at all. And they collected a lot of money inside. Doing things like this made them realise even more how lucky they both were. They were very spoilt and were given pretty much everything they wanted. But they also knew they had a lot to be grateful for.

CHAPTER 8

A few months later, Gabby and Florence were on their way to a hunter trials competition; this is riding and jumping across the country. They were competing in a pair's class, which meant they had to ride around together and jump around the course. Certain fences on the course are called 'dressing fences' which meant they had to be jumped side by side.

As they set off, Gabby and Florence jumped as they should but somehow on the way to the next fence, Gabby started falling; she was hanging by her ankle which had got stuck in her stirrup. Misty continued to canter along and Gabby was being dragged along until her leg twisted and she dropped to the ground. The competition was stopped so that there weren't any more people starting behind them.

The doctor came over in a Land Rover and as he walked up to Gabby, he said 'Okay young man, what have you done?'

Gabby was mortified. She looked at him, shocked, and told him she was a girl.

The doctor helped her up, put her in the back of the Land Rover and drove to the top of the hill.

He examined her leg and told her to sit in her
dad's Land Rover and rest it for a bit but it was
only twisted. This left Walter and Florence to get
the horses sorted out. The doctor said he would
come back soon but he was also competing that
day with his daughter so they had to wait until
he came back. Gabby sat in the front of the Land
Rover, her leg feeling strange and numb.
The swelling was massive. When the doctor
came to have another look, he said he thought
Walter needed to take her to the accident and
emergency department. On hearing this, Gabby
was insistent that she wanted to go home before
to change into a skirt as she didn't want the
doctor to see her knickers. She sat still whilst
Florence and Walter got the horses out of the
box and left them in clean beds and then Walter
drove them home.
When they got there, Walter carried Gabby out
and Yvette looked on in shock. Walter was
telling her what had happened whilst they were
dashing about trying to get the jodhpurs off and
put a skirt on. Then off to the hospital.
After a huge wait in the accident and emergency
department, Gabby was told she had broken her
leg and came out of the hospital with a plaster
from her foot all the way to the top of her leg.
Gabby was given crutches to get about on.
She was gutted but she also found out that you
can still ride with a plaster on.

Walter put her on Cardock as he was the most sensible and they went for a hack. Obviously not to be recommended.

CHAPTER 9

In September 1990, Gabby and Florence started Drover Field College, which was an agricultural college. This was where they were to stay for three years, studying for the British Horse Society Assistant Instructors Certificate and the Advanced National Certificate in Equine Business Management.

On starting the course, they didn't know anyone. They were shown around and both had a nice room each. They were so used to sharing at home, so they spent most of their time in Florence's room. They took Misty and Cardock with them so they could learn with them. They were going to be used as college horses as this was a cheaper way for them to take them along. Gabby found this hard to start with. She felt sick when people rode Misty and she could see them hanging on to her mouth but she soon got used to it and realised Misty wasn't going to take any grief from anyone. She certainly took her feisty attitude with her.

Gabby and Florence made a lot of friends at college. In their first year, it was all very new and scary.

They studied like mad, as this was for once in their lives something they had chosen to do. As time went by, they made even more friends and their confidence grew. They settled down more and starting going out and joining in with the college discos and sports.

During that first year, they were trying to get up to the farm where the horses were located where they were due to have an exam. Having recently passed their driving tests they were lucky; one of the farming lads loaned them his Morris Minor. On putting the key in, they discovered too late that the car had an alarm. It was very loud and was heard by everyone in classrooms nearby. They eventually figured out how to turn it off and drove to the exam, getting there just in time.

Whilst at college, they had various yard duties. It was on a rota system. They would either be on morning or evening duties.

This changed every week. Gabby loved doing the morning duties. She would get up early, go to the yard with the other girls and start mucking out.

She had two horses to look after; one of them was Misty.

She then had to groom them both to make them presentable for being ridden that day.

These were checked by the yard manager and anything that wasn't done to the standard she was expecting it had to be done again.

Then they would all have to tidy the yard and the horses would then be fed. After that, they'd leave the yard, go back to the dormitory and get changed into the clothes for the day's lessons. And go for breakfast.

For evening duties, you had to give the horses a good strapping, which is to groom them thoroughly, clean the tack of the horses in their care, skip out and tidy up the stables, ensure they have fresh hay nets, and then the yard gets tidied up again Then they would feed them again and make sure they had enough fresh water.

When they were on morning duties, they could finish at the end of the day after lessons and then relax and get their written work done so they'd then have a lovely long evening doing whatever they wanted. Gabby loved to go down to the college common room where the bar was open and she discovered she liked cider. She would get a drink, watch some football or a film or play some pool with the other students.

When it was half-term, Gabby and Florence had a day clinic with the event rider Suzanne Jenner; she was Gabby's favourite rider. She was like a celebrity to them. They had a friend take them there in his lorry. They had to work on cross-country that day. Misty was always excited when out with other horses and Gabby rode her in a vulcanite Pelham, so she could then be sure to have the brakes when needed.

That day, Gabby decided to try her in a snaffle which was much softer on her mouth, to see how she got on. They were all taken to the different fences on the course and instructed on how to jump them and what route was the best approach.

Gabby was leading the way on this and Misty was amazing; she went over everything she was asked. Suzanne asked her if there was anything she had issues with and for her, it was ditches. Misty would normally slam on the brakes. On the course, they had a coffin to jump, which is a jump, a ditch and then another jump. Gabby rode positively and Misty went straight through, popped over the fences and the ditch with no hesitations. Apparently, Misty was fine with ditches that day.

They went down some huge steps, which Gabby had never done before, they had to go into a wooded area, jump out of the woods and then straight down four steps.

Misty handled them really well. They then moved on to a bank where they had to jump up a bank, over a fence at the top and then jump off. Misty went up, jumped the fence but was not happy about jumping off. Gabby sat using lots of les and a few slaps of the whip but she was digging her heels in.

Suzanne came up to the bank to try to encourage her from behind.

And after some shouting and arm waving, she finally jumped off. That was the sticky fence that day. She was a brilliant horse; Gabby was so proud of her. She was beaming when they got back to the lorry and was so happy about how the day had gone, she spent most of the journey chatting about each fence and how wonderful Misty had been.

CHAPTER 10

Gabby loved Misty so much and wouldn't hear a
bad word said against her. If anyone was going
to walk past her stable, she would always tell
them to make sure they get off the concrete as
they go past and then back on after as Misty
wouldn't hesitate in launching herself at them
with her teeth. On one occasion, Florence was
walking past her and Misty bit a chunk off her
finger.

Another time when Misty was out in the field,
Walter was also out in the field picking up
droppings with a wheelbarrow. It's one of the
things they were very strict on at keeping the
field clean. Misty saw Walter, walked over to
him, bit his back and then ran off. Luckily, even
though it was a summer day, it wasn't warm
and Walter had a wax jacket on. Even through
the jacket she had cut the skin. She was a real
cheeky character and liked to see what she could
get away with. She was a bit like a naughty
child.

During the holidays from college, Gabby and
Florence would farm sit for some friends and
they would feed the dogs, muck out and feed the
horses.

They would go back to the house and get themselves some breakfast and then they would clean the whole house before going out to ride the horses. The house was a lovely big farmhouse, surrounded by fields.

They also had the use of the Range Rover which Gabby really enjoyed. They would take it out to go and check on their own horses and sort them out in between doing things at the farm. They also had to keep an eye on the cows, which never caused any problems.

The dogs that were there were well-behaved Labradors but had the most foul-smelling food. The dogs were so eager to get the food they would have to shut them in one room whilst getting it ready and then put the food down in the boot room which is where they had to be fed, and then once out of the way, they would open the door to let the dogs through. They ate so fast that it didn't touch the sides. In true Labrador fashion.

The two horses were lovely to ride. They took them out on hacks or in the field where the cows were and then through to another where they could take them for a gallop. They were a pleasure to look after and it felt like they lived on the farm. It was such fun to do and it was so nice to be entrusted to look after all these animals and the wonderful house.

Whilst they were at the farm, they sat in the kitchen one evening; it was lovely and cosy in there. They had a window seat and a lovely large wooden table. The dogs would be lying on the floor and they would have the television on in the background. Out the window, they noticed a motorbike that kept going past. They would see it go past slowly and the person riding would be looking in. Then it would go past again. They would hear it flying up the road then it would come back. They had a look out and Gabby went outside to see who it was. It was a lad from near where they lived and it was obvious to her that he knew they were there. He spotted Gabby in the gateway and gave her a smile. Then drove off. Gabby hadn't seen a smile like it and the lad's eyes were stunning. She felt weak at the knees. He was definitely someone she'd look out for.

CHAPTER 11

Back at college, they were fitting in just fine. It was like being in a family with all their new friends. At the end of the days, they would all sit out in the corridors and do homework or just chat. In the first year, they were in the girl's block because they were under 18.

Being at agricultural college, they used to go to the young farmer's parties, which all went on till the early hours. That would mean dashing back to college and climbing through a lecture room window to make it back to their bedrooms without being caught.

College discos were always good too, they would be able to drink, and then just walk back to their beds. Drover Field College was amazing; it seemed a world away from living at home. It also gave them a certain amount of freedom which they were not used to.

Each morning, they would get dressed and go into the common room and see which horses they were riding morning and afternoon and what kind of lesson they would be having; jump, flatwork, cross-country etc.

It always made Gabby giggle when she saw a certain friend's name down to ride Misty.

Misty was always very naughty for her and tried to scare her on as many opportunities as possible.

Generally, they had a good mix of college horses to ride and the instructors were all fantastic and worked them all hard to get to the standard required to pass their exams.

They also had to study the theory side and there was a classroom in the yard, which was where the previous exam was held. They had a lot of coursework to do and it mostly had to be written, so it took quite some time.

Lots of girls went out with the farming lads. It was a great time. Gabby spotted a boy she found attractive. His name was Tom. She used to see him on morning yard duties and they'd smile at each other, and he asked her out. She was so happy about it but also scared. She'd never had a boyfriend before. She originally said yes but the thought made her nervous.

They spent a lot of time just flirting and during that time they had a grand opening of the college's new indoor school.

All the equestrian students had to do different demonstrations. The farming students came to watch and Tom was one of them.

He was making it obvious that he was there to watch her and not bothered about the actual opening event.

This was as far as they went, nothing more than flirting. It was not the right time. She was worried that her dad would find out that she had a boyfriend when he said they should be studying.

Time went by and the riding and studying was good. Gabby was really enjoying the work. One evening, all the girls went down to the common room after finishing the coursework they had to do that night. The football was on that night, so she decided to get a drink and sit and watch. As she sat down, she noticed a boy who was really good looking, totally into the football, but started to speak to her. She found him easy to talk to. His name was Noah, he was from Manchester and he was on the farming course. She was so excited meeting him and couldn't figure out how she hadn't seen him before. He asked her out and Gabby again was torn. She really wanted to say yes to him but she felt shy and had no experience with boys so she said no. She felt terrible. She'd say to her friends, 'What is wrong with me? Why can't I give it a go?' It made her unhappy for quite a while. Gabby decided the best thing to do was to just carry on with her work and forget about boys to have as boyfriends.

CHAPTER 12

On her middle year of college, it was a gap year, where the girls all went out to different professional yards. Gabby and Florence went to a Dressage yard as this was the discipline they were not so keen on. They thought this would help them learn more and improve jumping for their own horses.

They worked for Julie Hardy. She was an FBHS, (Fellow of the British Horse Society). This is the highest level of instructor you can get. She was an amazing rider. Gabby learnt a lot from training with her. They would get to the yard in the mornings, muck out their delegated horses then go into the house to have breakfast. They'd discuss what was happening that day then get ready to go out on exercise. If someone was coming for a lesson, they would get the horse ready for the pupil.

Some days, Julie would have people come to her to be trained in dressage judging.

They all had to quickly learn a dressage test, then all ride it on the horses against their names for the person to judge.

It was something she enjoyed doing, they still all got competitive and it was a lot of fun.

Gabby realised that the flat work she was learning with Julie was something that she started to enjoy and also that it wasn't just boring circles. Julie showed them how important it was and how much better the horses can compete over jumps when they get the flat work right.

Gabby and Florence also did teaching on their year out. They taught the children in the villages surrounding them. It was rewarding to see the children start trotting, cantering and popping over jumps.

CHAPTER 13

Going back to college for their third year was a bit like starting all over again. Lots of new people and the whole place felt different. Gabby was so happy to be back there amongst her friends. This was the year Gabby was studying for her Advanced National Certificate in Equine Business Management. It was an interesting course which involved a lot of written work as well as the riding. They were taught how to run an equestrian centre and they had to write up a business plan for this and then for the following year after it had opened, they had to show what they had done; showing a profit. It was a lot of work to do.

The yard duties continued and when not working in theory lessons or riding; Gabby discovered more about the social side of things. Gabby spent a lot of time with her friend Ginny and they would spend a lot of time with Logan. Florence had a boyfriend called Mark at the time and he was best friends with Logan. So that meant they spent a lot of time hanging out. They played twister a lot and after having a few drinks in the common room, it was even more hilarious.

One night, they sat in Logan's room and watched The Crays film. The rooms in the boy's block smelt like sheep, pigs and cows. On looking back when Gabby smells one of those smells; it all comes flooding back. Logan would go to Gabby's room and sit on her bed. They'd listen to music and chat. They loved spending time together and he was easy to talk to. He also had a twin.

Logan took Gabby and Florence to his home one evening. They met his parents who were really lovely. Logan's mum said she knew they were from a good family because they had clean shoes on. Logan also took them to meet his sister who was working behind a bar at that time. They stopped for a drink and met Ali who was lovely. She was busy but it was nice to meet the person Gabby had heard so much about.

Gabby fancied Logan, he was fun, easy to talk to and she went weak at the knees whenever she saw him. He had a girlfriend at the time, so it was just a dream. So, Gabby had to make do with friendship. She hoped that one day they would become closer. She had a feeling Logan liked her too. He would come out to clubs with them and then have to dash off. So his girlfriend didn't know he'd been with her.

Logan took her to his parent's farm on a different day and took her out on his quad bike. Gabby was excited at the thought of it.

She had to get on the back of the bike and hold on to Logan to keep on the bike. She felt her heart beat faster being so close and being able to touch him. He drove them very fast out of the farmyard and took them down a lane. He was hurtling along and spun round to go back to the farm. Gabby was holding on for dear life, not wanting Logan to know how scared she was. They got off and laughed their heads off.
You could tell from the cheeky look on Logan's face that he had gone like a bat out of hell on purpose. Gabby was looking at him, wondering if he did it to make her hold on tighter. Logan's mum made them a drink and they sat in the lovely farmhouse kitchen drinking tea. It was such a comfortable home. It felt homely and Gabby was always made to feel really welcome. Whilst they were having their tea, Gabby was chatting with Logan's mum and she'd see him looking at her. When she looked at him, there was a brief moment when their eyes locked and then she turned away and carried on chatting. Then it would happen again. This was making Gabby wonder what was going on in his mind. Did he like her too?
They finished their tea and went out to get back to college.
Logan said he needed to go in one of the outbuildings and asked her to go with him.

She went in and as she got in there, Logan kissed her. It was what she'd been wanting for so long. She didn't want it to end. She wanted to hold on to him and make it last forever but suddenly the door opened and Logan's dad walked in which made them pull apart.

They both went out of the room and did not say a word about what had happened. Gabby was thinking, was this her imagination? Would this happen and please, let this happen again. They drove back to college together and chatted about the usual college stuff and Gabby told Logan how much she'd enjoyed the evening.

One day, they were on the farm together again. Logan had to go outside and help his dad and Gabby was chatting to his mum. She asked her to promise to always look after him for her. Gabby promised she always would. This meant a lot to her to think his mum trusted her to care for him. She would never forget that request and would always keep to her word.

CHAPTER 14

Whilst Gabby and Florence were at college, their parents bought them a car. This made getting to the farm a lot easier. It also made socialising a lot more possible. They took it in turns driving at night so they could have a drink. They would cram as many people in the car as possible.
One night, there was a young farmer's party and they went along. Florence had a new boyfriend at that time, Jacob; he was a farming student. A really nice lad. Logan came along to the party with them, along with some of Jacob's friends. It was quite a drive and Florence was in the front and Jacob was driving. Gabby was in the back along with two other people they didn't know. Being so close in the car, Gabby was finding it hard to breathe with Logan's legs touching hers and didn't dare look over. She didn't know what to do with her hands as when she tried putting them on her lap they would drift and nearly touch Logan's leg. It was torture. Was Logan feeling the same? He certainly didn't move away from being so close together. He was no longer dating the girl he'd been seeing. He and Gabby had continued to spend time together but they hadn't mentioned the kiss.

On the journey, the mood in the car was excited and happy. Everyone was really looking forward to a good night. When they got there, it was in a huge barn. It was absolutely packed. They went in and got themselves a drink. Gabby stood drinking her drink and watching people dancing and looking around to see who she recognised. She saw Florence and Jacob chatting and laughing with some other people she didn't know. Probably Jacob's friends. Gabby saw some people she knew from other young farmers' parties and had a few chats. She was wondering where Logan had gone and found somewhere to put her drink. She stood by the wall and was going back over the journey in the car and how much she'd hoped he'd put his arm around her. She jumped when she got a tap on the arm. It was Logan; he said 'What are you doing here on your own?'

Gabby said she was just watching people. He was acting different to normal. He asked her to dance with him. It was an upbeat tune so she said yes. They got on the dance floor and had fun messing around. She was enjoying this time they were spending together. Then the song finished and the DJ put on a slow song. Logan looked at Gabby. It was a look that made her heart skip. She didn't want to move. He stepped forward and asked her to dance. She didn't say anything, just stepped forward and he held her close.

She put her arms around him and they danced together, they talked for a bit and then just danced and held each other close. The song was coming to an end and Gabby really didn't want to let go. They stopped and looked into each other's eyes, the music finished and another slow song came on. They remained in each other's arms and standing there, it felt like they were the only ones in the room. Logan leaned towards Gabby and kissed her. She was in heaven. This had been what she'd hoped to feel again. This time, it wasn't stopped midway. They were kissing for a long time, it was passionate and Gabby's head felt dizzy with the emotion of it.

They only stopped when they realised the music had changed to a dance tune and Logan lead Gabby away from the dance floor. She walked with him, holding his hand and he led her outside.

Logan said 'I can't tell you how long I've wanted to do that for. I've always worried that if I made a move, it would ruin our friendship. I was torn to know what to do but, in the end, I had to try.' Gabby had a big smile on her face. She said, 'you have no idea how much I've wanted you to say that. I've had the biggest crush on you since we started college.'

It was the best feeling in the world.

They moved closer together now and kissed again; this time it was passionate and they both found themselves holding on tight. They stayed outside for the rest of the evening, sat on some steps, talking, hands linked together, and they discussed the feelings they had and that they'd both been unsure of whether to say anything. It felt so good to know they both felt the same. When the party had finished, Florence and Jacob found them sitting outside. They seemed surprised to see Gabby and Logan together and said 'Finally, what took you so long?'
They all laughed.

CHAPTER 15

Work continued and Gabby studied hard. She found her new feelings of happiness after that night made her feel more positive and focused for the future. They had a famous rider coming to the college to teach them. The lady, Violet Brown, was a famous show-jumper who represented Great Britain many times. Gabby loved those sessions. Violet liked Misty. She got so much encouragement and Violet would put the jumps higher and higher. Misty flew over them all with ease.

When Violet came a few months later, Gabby couldn't afford to join the sessions but Misty was down to be ridden by her friend Eve. Eve wasn't a fan of Misty and Misty knew it. That day, they watched the tuition. Violet put up a double, where you had one stride in between. The jumps were right up the side of the indoor school where Gabby was sitting with the other girls from the course.

Eve had a trot round, cantered in the corner and came round to the first fence.

Misty jumped the first and got to the second; she went to jump it but changed her mind.

Eve shot up Misty's neck. This is where she stayed whilst Misty proceeded to trot around the indoor school. Misty knew exactly what she was doing. From their seats in the viewing gallery, the girls had to stifle giggles. Misty was being her true cheeky self and thankfully, Eve didn't get hurt.

Twice a week as part of the training, they would travel to a local riding school for practical and theory lessons from other qualified instructors. All the girls and one boy were not keen on these times. When they got to the school, they had to go to the tack room and check which horse they were riding. The name they all dreaded seeing next to their own name was Nilo. He was a huge dark grey, heavy horse. He had massive feet like dinner plates and he felt like you were riding a tank. He was solid and very unpredictable. Gabby saw her name next to his and felt sick. She chatted to her friends and they said they should all refuse to ride him but there wasn't time to have the discussion properly so she had to just go with it.
She took his tack and a grooming kit. He was so big that she could hardly reach to put his saddle on. Once she'd got him ready, she led him out into the yard and lined up. Her feet only just went past the saddle flaps, which explained a little of how large he was.

They all had to mount together then ride out to the outdoor school. Gabby got on and was determined to keep control. She followed everyone who rode in the line into the school. They were told to ride around and warm up. The instructor then said, 'Right we're going out in the field.'

Gabby couldn't believe her ears. She really didn't want to take this horse in a field. She'd managed to ride around without incident in the school which in her mind was a miracle because only the week before he'd taken off in that same outdoor school and landed on one of her friends. They all filed out of the gate and made their way across a field and into the field where they were to ride. The instructor told them all to do some flatwork, so everyone started schooling the horses they were riding. Gabby took Nilo up the top of the field to a flat area; she was trotting him round in a circle trying to get him to bend around her leg. Just as she rode past the instructor, the instructor threw a log into the hedge. Nilo bolted. He went at a flat-out gallop towards the hedge.

Gabby sat back and was trying desperately to stop him.

She thought he was about to jump but she managed to turn him away.

Just when she thought that was a close one, he bolted again.

He didn't stop this time and went careering downhill towards the gate. It was a large field and Gabby tried to sit up and get back control but he had pulled his head right down and had absolutely no intention of stopping. At the gate, he stopped. It was horrible. She sat there in shock.

Her instructor shouted to 'Come back at once.' Gabby replied, 'I'm not coming back.'

She did start making her way back to the top of the hill; half-halting all the way up. The ride had stopped and everyone came in close together. The instructor told her to get off and swap with another girl. She didn't need asking twice. She swapped with her friend. Gabby got on to a horse she hadn't ridden before but something a whole lot safer.

Her friend Justine got her foot in the stirrup and Nilo bolted again. She went hurtling round the field. It was horrendous to watch. When Justine tried to turn him, he fell over and knocked her hard onto the ground, then he took off, reins flapping around. Justine was lying on the ground and was knocked out.

Gabby sat there in horror as it all happened. And felt so terribly guilty for swapping. Justine was taken to the hospital and treated for a concussion. The girls all took it in turns to take care of her and kept going in her room to check on her. It was a frightening day for them all.

Gabby and Florence had a great year that year and had gone through the work and exams, but thought their partying may well have stopped them from passing their exams. On the day of the results, they were both told they had passed. They had to run up to the village and call their parents to say they did actually have to go to the prize giving after all.

The day of leaving college was awful, Gabby felt so sad. She had loved it there and it had felt like home and she was going to miss her friends so much.

Gabby and Logan didn't know what would happen between them with them living so far away from each other. Gabby was looking at jobs in yards near to him but her parents wanted the girls to stay together, so she declined. The budding romance dwindled and they remained friends but continued with their own lives.

CHAPTER 16

Being back at home, Gabby and Florence joined the local young farmers. It was a smallish club and they made lots of friends. There was always lots going on. During that time, the girls decided to move out from their parents' place. They moved into a mobile home which Walter had bought and put in the barn, with half of it sticking out. It was very old but they loved it and it gave them the independence they were used to after being in college.

They didn't have any electricity in the mobile home, so they took a big extension lead, plugged it in in the tack room and then poked it through one of the windows of the mobile home. This allowed them to have a two-ringed cooker and a heater. They had to go to the tack room to wash and go to their parents for showers but this was fine. They were both happy living like that. When it rained, they had to go to the sitting area because the bedroom leaked. It was all fun though and they had lots of people stay over on the floor after parties.

One night, they had a young farmer's party to go to and Gabby was having fun dancing with the other girls. She noticed a boy looking over at her. He came over and asked her to dance. She accepted and his eyes took her breath away. It was the boy she'd spotted all those years before with the amazing eyes. He smelt lovely and Gabby suddenly thought things were looking up. His name was Owen. He lived in the next village to them. He was 17 and she was 20. Gabby did wonder about the age gap but to her, it didn't matter. He asked her out and Gabby said yes.

She would go to work, and then in the evenings they would get together or go out somewhere. She really wanted to be able to be open about being with him but was scared about what her parents would think. They had all been invited to a garden party by the people who lived next door so Gabby decided that would be a good place for them to meet. Neutral ground. They all went along. Walter was very protective and Gabby was worried it would scare Owen off. The meeting went well and he passed what felt like a vetting.

After that, they went out and about, had lots of fun.

He was her first proper boyfriend and she was really scared about getting it all right.

It was an overwhelming feeling. She was falling for him and from how it was going she was hoping he felt the same. They got so close but there was still the niggling worry in the background of Walter coming along to tell them off. It was really putting a spanner in the works. One evening, they went to a nightclub – they drove there. Gabby and Owen were in the front and Florence was with her boyfriend, Dylan in the back. Both of the lads wanted them to stop. They stopped at a cafe and decided to just go back to Dylan's house. When they got there, Florence and Dylan went into his room and Gabby and Owen stayed downstairs. Owen said he had something for her and gave her a beautiful silver necklace. He put it on her and she had never been given anything so beautiful before.

Gabby had fallen in love with him and one evening whilst they were together he said he'd have spoken to his dad and because of the way her own dad was, that he thought they'd better call it a day. She was heartbroken. She couldn't blame him, with her protective dad looming over them. But she loved him so much. After that, she kept away from boys for a long time. She felt like her heart had been ripped out. He was her first real love.

Going to young farmers or just the pub was tricky after that, as they would see each other and all she wanted to do was to go and tell him how much she thought of him and to sort things out, but it never happened. He was going to be a hard act to follow, that was for sure.

After that, they went to the cinema and they all went as they had before. Owen was back to his cheeky self and was sat at the back throwing popcorn down at them all.

One night when they were out, they decided to move someone's car as a joke. One of their friends had a car that had dodgy brakes so they all managed to move the car into a different parking place. When they all came out of the cinema, she was panicking that her car had been stolen and they were all trying not to laugh knowing fully well where the car was. After she spotted it two cars away, she laughed and realised what had happened.

CHAPTER 17

They all went out into one of the neighbouring villages one night. Gabby and her friends were out, a lot of the young farmers, and also some of the other lads from the next village. Gabby realised Owen was there and still had feelings for him but didn't want him to think she was following him. She also felt like making him jealous. She decided to have some fun.

She saw a lad that she did quite fancy and who also was not that friendly with Owen. She made sure she gave him lots of attention and he really made her laugh. He was older than her and she knew his brothers too. He said he wasn't staying too late out because of work but that was before the pub crawl began.

They went from pub to pub and finally, time was getting on and the pubs were starting to shut. That was when Luke asked her if she could possibly drive his car back for him. He'd had too much to drink to drive back. Gabby wasn't drinking so she said yes straight away. It was a huge honour because Luke was very precious about his car and wouldn't let anyone drive it.

She was happy to think he trusted her to drive it, even though it was probably more likely that he didn't want to leave it parked up somewhere other than outside his own home at night. But this didn't worry her. Gabby told Florence she was going to drive his car back and she could follow-on and pick her up. Florence was also not drinking so she drove back with a group of people in their car and Gabby got into Luke's car.

As she did this though Owen decided he wanted a lift by her. It was a tricky situation. Luke said it was ok and so Owen got in the car as well as a friend of Luke's and then Luke got in the front with Gabby in the driving seat. Gabby could see that Owen was looking at her in the rear-view mirror and she tried not to let him know she was looking at him.

She was thinking, is he in here wanting her back? Was it just because she was in Luke's car and he just doesn't want her with him? Please god, let it be that he wants her back. She drove back in what felt like awkward stilted conversations. The lads obviously didn't like each other and Gabby kept trying to add a few jokey comments to diffuse the situation.

She got to Owen's house to drop him off and he reluctantly got out of the car.

She looked at him and he looked at her with a strange look in his eyes, turned and walked into his house without looking back. Gabby then thought, right that's how it is, so she put the car into gear and drove off towards Luke's house. She thought Florence must be about to catch up with them soon. She stopped past the pub and Luke's friend who had been sat in the back got out and went down the lane to his house. Then Gabby continued to Luke's house where she stayed waiting for Florence to come and get her. Luke said thank you for driving his car back and for not damaging it.

As they were waiting, Luke leant forward and kissed her. Gabby was thrown to start with, surprised at the sudden contact, but she didn't push him away. He stopped when he heard a car coming and round the corner drove Florence. Gabby didn't say anything other than, 'See you sometime,' and left.

CHAPTER 18

As Gabby and Florence turned 21, they decided to organise a party. They didn't want grown-ups or any parents going. This was just to be a party for friends. They invited all the young farmers and most of the young people around the surrounding villages. They organised a disco and asked the local pub in Perringhill to do the bar for them.

It took a while for people to start arriving and they were nervous that nobody would turn up, but they did. It was a really great party. Everyone really enjoyed themselves and there wasn't a sober person in the room. Gabby actually managed to take photos of the party, none of which were of her or Florence. After most parties, they had people staying in the mobile home with them, crashing out on the floor or sofa bed or anywhere there was a space, and this was no exception. Luke and Jack stayed over that night. The next morning, Luke drove them both to the village hall to clean it up and collect their things along with their car.

That afternoon, they had a tug-of-war for young farmers.

Everyone had huge hangovers and were feeling very delicate. Some had dark glasses. They had lots of gossip about who had done what that night. It was going to be one of those parties that were remembered as one of the greats.

CHAPTER 19

After leaving college, Gabby and Florence
decided to find a job at a yard rather than teach
full-time. They went for an interview at a yard
close by for a lady called Stella. She lived in a
beautiful house with lovely stables and gardens,
a good size outdoor school, and lots of fields.
The interview went well and she took them both
on.
When they got there in the mornings, they
would feed the horses and then start mucking
them out. By the time the mucking out was
done, they had to get the horses ready to be
ridden. Some days, Stella would want to go out
on exercise too. After mucking out, she very
often invited the girls in for a cup of tea and
gave them the rundown of what she wanted
them to do that day. The horses were fantastic
and no expense was spared. They all had the
best of everything. They had to just take the
horses out walking to start with and work up to
trot, canter and then schooling and jumping
ready for the hunting season. It was a lot of
strict exercise to get the horses all to peak fitness.

Gabby loved Stella's horses. They were all so nice to ride and the location of Stella's home was so close to lots of off-road tracks and fields they could go out on.

Some days, they would go out on exercise in the morning and then go out and do some flatwork or some jumping in the afternoon.

Stella had a young, Irish Draught cross horse called Hurricane; who she wanted to show. He was huge and really didn't know his own strength. Gabby would try leading him in the field to get him used to a head collar and he'd jump around, legs flying all over the place. They spent quite some time with him, getting him used to people and how to behave. When they took him to competitions, he did very well.

A huge perk of the job was having lessons with Bryn Dyer. Bryn was an event rider who became the British Olympic Team Trainer. He was brilliant, and on a few nice summer days, he would come and teach them. So, all the horses benefitted from his instruction as Gabby and Florence rode along with Stella and her daughter, Hazel. He had a way of telling you to do things that helped make jumping effortless. Gabby was in heaven during those lessons. She wanted to make the most of the opportunity they were given. He was someone she could learn so much from and she intended on being fully aware of everything he was telling them to soak up all the knowledge he was passing on.

Part of working with Stella meant they also had hound puppies to walk for The Anbury Vale Hunt. They were situated just up the road from her house. They had a male and female puppy and they were kept in a huge kennel with a run. They had to keep the kennels clean, feed them and take them out for walks. They were fun to take out; both hounds were very boisterous. The male, more so. He was strong-willed and wanted to work from very small. He went on to become a very good working hound. The female unfortunately was not so lucky. She was a beautiful-looking hound. She was gentle and would like to try snuggling up to you, which wasn't the type of hound they needed. She didn't make it on to the hunting field.

The hours working for Stella were long. They both had to get up at 4 am and do their own horses and then drive to Stella's to start their job. In the hunting season, they would have to be up for the first horses to go, and then exercise, get the second horses ready and drive them up to where Stella could change her horse. Some days that was a real adventure trying to find them and also somewhere to park a trailer on the side of the road. They found it exciting, and they would get to meet up with the other grooms. When they got back from hunting, they would have to wash the horses off, feed them, skip out the others and then clean all the tack.

One evening, Stella was having a dinner party and asked if Florence and Gabby would stay on to waitress for her. They agreed and it was a lot of fun. She always had very well-attended and very good parties.

Stella's daughter Hazel had just got a new horse and had arranged to take it to have tuition going round an event course. On that day, Stella said that Gabby and Florence could share one of her horses and go around the course too. Gabby knew the lady teaching as she met her when she had been an examiner at one of her teaching exams. They all got to ride around the whole course and jump all the different fences. This was another golden opportunity given to them by Stella. There are not many owners that would allow their grooms to go and join in like they were allowed to.

CHAPTER 20

Gabby and Florence decided they wanted to go to a new yard after some time and work in a discipline they had not been involved in before. A friend of theirs told them a local polo yard was looking for people, so they went along to have a chat and see if this was what they were looking for and if the employers were happy for them to work for them. They both got offered a job. At the time, they needed one person to work with their hunters and another to do the polo ponies. Gabby looked after the polo ponies and Florence looked after the hunters.

As it was February, the polo ponies were still out at grass, but there were a few in who had different ailments that needed treating daily. Gabby would also have to walk around the field and tidy up the rugs on the others and check the horse's legs and feet. Gabby was paid £45 a week and she loved every minute of it.

After a while, they started bringing in more grooms and they had a lot of work to do to prepare for the day when all the ponies were being brought in.

It started snowing when they were trying to get the beds down and it was very slippery underfoot. One of the tack rooms needed cleaning out and Gabby and a lad called Ryan had to clear it out. They were trying to move a sofa, which was old and rotting.

As Ryan and Gabby tried to move it, something shot out. To Gabby's horror, a huge rat came running towards her. It ran straight into her leg. She screamed and ran out of the door. Both of them were now not keen on going back in there to get the sofa out but they had a job to do. Finally, after some pushing and shoving, back and forth, they got the sofa out of the tack room and put it on the bonfire.

When the ponies came in, the grooms were all split into yards and they all had their own ponies to look after. Gabby was sharing a yard with Adam. They both got on really well. Gabby was given ponies for two owners. Her favourite pony was called Joy, she belonged to Rupert King. She was a sensitive type and very gentle; she was also very fast. Her other ponies belonged to Dominic Clarke; he would come down after work to ride.

Gabby had to get the ponies ready and take them down to the field and meet him. He would ride around and practice stick and ball, in the chukka field. Gabby was lucky, both of the owners she worked for were lovely and always thanked her for what she did for them.

A great thing about this job was they were allowed to take their dogs to work with them. Stella also let them do that, whilst working for her. Gabby loved having her dog with her. She was a Jack Russell crossed with a Norfolk terrier, called Dash. She went to work with Gabby every day and was able to run around and had so much freedom. Florence had Dash's sister who was called Whisper. She also went to work with them both.

Gabby had to be careful with Dash as she was very cheeky and loved playing with balls. This could be tricky working on a polo yard and she had to be locked in the tack room when the ponies were being taken down to the chukka field or for matches so she didn't chase the ball. At the main yard, there were school ponies there where people would come and have lessons on how to play polo. The polo school was pretty busy and they had Grayson and Evan teaching. Grayson was one of the owners of the yard and Evan was a rider/groom. He played polo himself. Evan was at a yard with Julia and they had to go out of the ground that the other yards were on and up the road a way.

Gabby and Evan were close. They spent a lot of time together. They would do the work as they should and Gabby learnt a lot from Evan.

He had been at pony club with both of the girls but they hadn't really come across each other before. Evan obviously liked Gabby and she'd make a point of being the first to volunteer to help at his yard if they needed someone. He was good fun and she went weak at the knees whenever she saw him. He was tall and good-looking, had sparkly eyes and a cheeky smile. She was well and truly smitten. Every day, she would look forward to going to work – not just for the ponies, but to be working with Evan. Working with the polo ponies was a busy job. They worked six very long days and had Mondays off. So, on Sunday nights, they would all meet at the pub. There was live music and they'd dance and drinks, then all go back to Evan's house.

When everyone was laughing and chatting in the lounge, Evan and Gabby would sneak off to be together. She thought this must be how it felt being truly happy. Being with the horses and working on a yard she loved and also being with someone she really cared about.

They had such a good life, riding during the days, going out with friends and going back to their own horses to take them out.

After work finished, before going back to their own horses, they'd all go to the field where the match had been held and have a cider with the other grooms and have a laugh together.

Idyllic doesn't come close to explaining how wonderful that world felt to Gabby.

CHAPTER 21

One weekend, Gabby and Florence had Lisa come and stay for the weekend. Lisa was a close friend from college and when Gabby asked Grayson if it was ok for her to work with them that weekend, he was more than happy.

Yvette said to Lisa, 'Don't be surprised if someone gets carted off in an ambulance.'

There seemed to be a lot of bumps and falls and the ambulance was a pretty regular sight.

It was 11th June 1995; they had a busy day ahead. It was the first match to be played that season on ground one. Gabby had to take all her ponies and also pick up another pony on the way which was for sale, and Dominic was going to try it out during the match.

She was feeling so happy that day. They had a full day of polo and then they had a big party arranged for after and she couldn't wait. She'd get to spend more time with Evan and she was so happy about that.

She rode down collecting another horse from a neighbouring yard which was for sale and was being tried out by Dominic that day.

She tied them all up and her owners had given her instructions on which pony they wanted for which chukka. All her ponies were well-behaved Gabby's first pony was out playing and she had to get her next pony ready, she was the horse that was for sale. Gabby had ridden her before and she'd had no problems. She was a chestnut mare around 16hh, called Ada. Tristan, who she belonged to, had said to her to make sure when she was about to mount to get on at the pony lines. Gabby did that and as soon as she sat down and walked a few steps, she could feel Ada was lame. With the chukka's being so short, they had to get things ready pretty quickly so she went to speak to her boss, Sadie. Gabby told her that Ada was lame and that she would double up on one of her ponies and explain to Dominic after the match finished.

Sadie told her to trot her up. Gabby went forward in to a trot and Ada gave a few little rears.

She was obviously uncomfortable and Gabby said to Sadie, 'Look, she's obviously not happy. I'm happy to take responsibility for the pony change. Dominic will understand. 'Sadie was not listening, she told Gabby to turn round and trot up again. Gabby turned poor Ada around and this time, Ada wasn't having any of it.

She reared up so high, she lost her balance and fell over backwards.

Gabby hit the ground, she was lying on the ground when Ada followed and landed on top of her.

Ada scrambled off Gabby and trod on her leg getting up. She then trotted off and a groom caught her. Gabby was screaming that she couldn't feel her legs. She was in so much pain. Sadie came over to her and said, 'Shut up Gabby. You're only bruised, stop making a fuss. There are lots of important people here today and everyone is watching. You're making a scene.'

Florence came over, distraught, and wanted to phone their parents but Sadie wouldn't let her use her phone, so she ran off to find someone that would.

In the meantime, Sadie sat Gabby up and took off her riding hat, chaps and boots. The chaps were zipped up around the back of her legs. Gabby was wearing jeans underneath.

By this time, the match had been halted and Grayson came running over to her. He looked at her and said 'Don't worry, you'll be okay'.

At that moment, Gabby knew something was really very wrong. She could tell by the look on his face. He had a kind manner and wanted to reassure her but she could tell from his expression he didn't think she was okay really. The paramedics drove over to where Gabby was laying on the ground.

As they were getting her on a spinal board, they were trying to decide if they needed an air ambulance. They decided on a slow ambulance. Yvette and Walter arrived as this was happening and emotions were running high. Gabby was still screaming and crying. Florence and Lisa were also in sheer terror. Yvette went in the ambulance with Gabby and Walter drove Florence and Lisa to the hospital.

When they were in the ambulance, Gabby said, 'Mum, I need a wee.'

Yvette didn't get to reply. The paramedic said to Gabby, 'Just go, we are used to cleaning up.' Gabby didn't manage it and the gravity of the situation was not yet sinking in.

When they reached the hospital, the staff gave Gabby some strong painkillers and they had to take x-rays and scans to ascertain what damage had been done. She was in shock and threw up everywhere when exiting the scanner. Things seemed to be happening. People were rushing around but Gabby felt like she was suspended in the air and had no control over what was going on. The doctor said they needed to operate.

CHAPTER 22

Gabby was in theatre for 9 hours, which was sheer hell for Yvette, Walter and Florence. Lisa had somehow managed to drive home in a haze. She had stayed up until Gabby went down to the theatre but then there was just the wait. She too was in shock like the family. All they had to do now was sit and wait.

The operation went well; the surgeon put in two rods and bolted them together with metal across. He said he had to put it in, otherwise she would never have been able to sit up again. She was given her own room in the hospital and Yvette and Florence took it in turns to stay overnight. As well as the operation on her back, the surgeons had to operate on her left leg too. The horse had trodden on Gabby's leg when she got up and broken both sides of her ankle.

The days went by in a blur; Gabby was given morphine to help her with the pain. At night, she was so uncomfortable and sore she would have her mum gently stroke her back for ages. It was soothing and helped Gabby to drift off to sleep. On the second week of being in the hospital, they allowed Gabby to get out of bed.

She wasn't able to move so the nurses would sit her on the side of the bed and drag her back under her arms into a wheelchair. When she was sat down, Yvette or Florence would take her out for some fresh air. They would walk down the road with her and sit outside with an ice lolly. Florence also suffered as a result of the accident. She went in to see Gabby most days and continued to work but she left the place of work where the accident was and went to work at Wrenbridge Hunt stables, where they had both done their work experience. She was happier there.

Walter and Yvette's time was taken up with the hospital visits and being with Gabby. Florence was left to go on with life and she didn't have the support that she needed. Gabby was getting all the attention and Florence was left to process all the trauma on her own.

CHAPTER 23

At the end of two weeks in the hospital, Gabby was in for a shock. She was given a place in a spinal unit. The nurses got her dressed and she was taken in an ambulance. The drivers didn't know the way to go without having to drive over speed bumps, so they had to follow Walter. Yvette went in the ambulance with Gabby. When they got to the hospital, the paramedics wheeled her out of the ambulance into the unit. The first thing Gabby saw was everyone was using wheelchairs. She was feeling very confused about what on earth was she doing there. She thought she must be at the wrong hospital. The hospital staff in the spinal unit were really strict. They were not happy that Gabby was dressed and dealt with that straight away.

She was given a room of her own and was told she had to stay alone. She wasn't allowed anyone staying in there with her. Gabby freaked, shouting and screaming at the doctors and nurses, crying loudly. This upset Yvette too who spoke to the nurses. They agreed she could stay one night but no more. Gabby was inconsolable. After this, the doctors came into the room.

They wanted to see which parts of Gabby's body she could feel and what kind of sensations she had. They had pins and would say 'sharp' or 'blunt' and she had to answer. When they got to certain areas, Gabby would be lying on the bed wondering if they were actually tricking her. She couldn't feel anything in lots of areas that they were poking and it was very distressing. Gabby was crying and Yvette was holding her hand trying to reassure her and trying to desperately hold it together for her daughter. This was a big deal and it was just the beginning.

The doctors left the room and again, Gabby broke down in tears. She felt desperately unhappy. What was going on? Was she having too much fun at polo? Why her? What had she done to end up like this?

When she was first in the spinal unit, she didn't want anything to do with any of the other patients. She said, 'I'm not like them. I'm not speaking to them.'

She insisted the door was kept closed all the time so she didn't have to see the wheelchairs going past. She changed after this; she turned in to an angry emotionally charged young girl.

She would think nothing of shouting at the doctors and nurses. She was a rude and really difficult patient.

She felt totally out of control. She had no way of getting out of bed. Her legs wouldn't move.

All the staff had routines for each of the patients and Gabby was going to be put through it whether she liked it or not.

At the time, they had a television celebrity who used to raise money for the unit. He would come around and meet all the new patients and their families. He was really good to Gabby and her family. He would come and sit on her bed and watch films with her. He'd often be seen walking around the hospital with a chicken drumstick in his hand. He lightened the mood and definitely helped Gabby with her anger and frustration.

CHAPTER 24

For Gabby, things got worse when the physio started. She was taken down and introduced to her physio. She had Yvette with her. Even though the hospital had said that Gabby was to stay in the hospital alone, Yvette came in without fail every day to stay with her. The first thing the physio had to teach Gabby was to sit up again. It was like being a rag doll. Like she was going to topple over at the slightest movement. Her physio had to put bean bags around her and had Yvette sit behind Gabby to stop her from falling. The physio would sit in front and throw a ball for Gabby to catch. She had to do this many times to get her balance. It took a long time to get this. She had to get used to moving herself in her bed. She was told she had to lift both legs separately and then move along. Gabby tried doing it but found her legs felt like a dead weight. She could see her mum watching, wanting to help but knowing it was something she had to let Gabby get on with. Gabby was getting annoyed with herself. It felt so difficult, how in the world was she ever going to be able to do this? When would things go back to normal?

This progressed to going on a tilt table. It was something you had to lie on, then be strapped in, and with a remote control, the physio would gradually tilt the table to a standing position. Gabby could see everyone around the room doing different kinds of work and it looked like hell. She felt it was like a torture chamber.

The next stage after the tilt table was something called a standing frame. This is a wooden frame where the patients are strapped in. They have to wheel inwards. The physio stands behind, the patient's feet go on the floor and one of the straps is put behind. The patient then has to reach forward to the table part of the frame and with the help of the physio, pull themselves up into the standing position. They would then have a strap under their bottom and one in front of the knees to stop them from falling.

Gabby had to line up and get into position for her first experience using a standing frame. She pulled herself up into the standing position, her physio strapped her in and said she'd be back in a while.

It was a very uncomfortable sensation. Gabby was fiercely trying to feel ok, but she was rapidly beginning to feel sick and her head started feeling like she was in fog. She fainted. She came round to being put in the wheelchair again and tipped back to get some blood flow back to her head.

As she had been in bed for so long without walking or standing, the shock to her body of her suddenly standing and allowing the blood to rush down to her feet made her faint. This was to happen quite regularly to her and to her fellow patients on the same journey.

CHAPTER 25

Depending on the level of one's injury, they have different abilities left and it differs in each person. Not one injury is the same. Gabby was paraplegic, which had left her paralysed from the waist down. Meaning she not only couldn't walk but she couldn't go to the toilet normally either.

Whilst Gabby was going through all of this rehabilitation, she had a catheter permanently in, so she didn't have to think about going for a wee but for her bowels she was given medication every night to make that work, then early in the morning the nurses would come round and put suppositories in all the patients whilst lying in bed, and they had protection on the beds. They were all then left for the suppositories to start working. This was for Gabby the worst part. She felt like she had no dignity left at all. It was a disgusting part of this injury. How could she even contemplate having to do this every day by herself?

She would go on to learn how to do this, manual evacuation as they called it in hospital.

This was taught whilst sitting on a toilet to make it as much as possible like normality.

She was also to learn how to use a catheter. The nurses took the permanent catheter out and Gabby had a humiliating lesson with a mirror and a catheter being taught where to put it in. She had such difficulty and it was worse that she was being taught on her bed with the curtains drawn, which at that stage was in a room of 6 beds, so whilst she was doing something so intimate and personal she could hear people chatting away in the room.

Another thing Gabby had to do was go to lectures. She felt like she was back at school. The lectures were held for people who were injured around the same time so they were all at roughly the same stage in their recovery. For Gabby, this meant she was the only girl in the group. The lectures were from how to look after your skin, which included how you wore clothes – all socks need to be inside out to avoid the pressure from the seam on your toes – to making sure you drink enough fluid, and keeping an eye on the colour of your urine. They had a talk on bowels, emptying them manually and ensuring this is regular. If you don't take care of this side, you can suffer badly from other illnesses, a stroke being one of them.

The chat you also had to take part in and for Gabby, it was mortifying, was the sex talk.

The blokes found it hilarious trying to work out how these things would work for them now. The blokes were laughing about taking Viagra to help them. Gabby sat there wondering how on Earth things would be for her now. How could she ever have a boyfriend, ever let anyone get close and see her like this? It was a really scary thought.

Gabby came out of that session really quiet. She knew the men had ways to make things work but had no idea how this would be for her in the future. She didn't say anything to Yvette but she was stuck on the thought of who would want her now? She had dreamt of having children one day but could that even happen now?

They said in the hospital that people do have children but the thought was terrifying to her.

CHAPTER 26

Each day was full of things to keep them busy.
Gabby did the sport she was down to try. She
enjoyed the basketball, was not keen on the
tennis, and the archery was hilarious. Arrows
went everywhere other than on the target. She
started to feel like she was in a community. It
was weirdly like being in some kind of club and
new family. As much as Gabby wanted to go
home, she couldn't imagine how she was going
to cope going home and not having any nurses
nearby.
Gabby was really lucky with friends, they still
came in every night and it was something she
enjoyed and looked forward to. Her fellow
patients enjoyed it too as they were all so good
at including everyone in the fun they brought in.

One evening, Gabby was listening to music and
had a Mars bar in her hand. She had been in
physio that day and also had a sports session so
was feeling like she'd had a tough day.
She fell asleep with the chocolate bar in her
hand.

On waking up, she was wondering what on Earth all the brown on her bed was and suddenly panicked that she'd had an accident until she realised that she had toffee stuck on her legs. She soon remembered the Mars bar. She quickly looked around to see if anyone else had spotted her looking at her bed with some concern. Everyone else was asleep, so she quickly got out of bed, pulled the covers across to cover it up and went to wash her things and clothes. Then she went to get showered and dressed and left to go to physio. She didn't say anything to anyone and by the time she came back to her bed, it had been changed to clean sheets. She told Yvette, who thought it was hilarious, but the nurses never mentioned it to her and she never said a word to them either. She was just hoping they realised it was actually chocolate and not something else.

One night she was having particular problems trying to sleep. She had problems getting in a good position. She would be ringing the bell to be asked for help. That night one of the larger, scarier nurses were on duty and she said to Gabby that she would go and make her some warm milk. She walked off to the nurse's kitchen and Gabby proceeded to fall asleep.

When the nurse went back to Gabby she leant over Gabby to hand her the milk and Gabby must have felt a presence next to her, woke with a start. She screamed, flung her arms out. Knocking the milk all over the nurse, the bed and herself. The nurse was not happy. She wiped up the milk from her uniform and dabbed at the bed with her tissue but snapped at Gabby for making a mess and told her to 'Now, go to sleep'. She left Gabby wet with milk and stomped off back to the nurse's station.

CHAPTER 27

Gabby got up one morning and found she was still in so much pain. She couldn't understand how this could be with her paralysed. Her doctor explained that because she had nerves that were damaged and sort of floating around, they don't know where to send the signals when there is a bump or an injury of any kind. If someone kicked an able-bodied person, they would know exactly what had happened and it would hurt but they'd generally rub it and the pain would subside, but for someone with a spinal cord injury it would be like their nerves scream and they feel it 10 times more than they would if they had normal sensation.

The doctor who spent so much time with her was there from the start and even though she gave him so much abuse, he still came back and made sure she was doing the right things. He never shouted at her. He was firm and wasn't going to stand for any disrespect. They were trying to help put Gabby's life back together and ensure she knew as much as possible about how to become independent again when she was discharged from the hospital.

Life had taken a nosedive and she was frightened for what may lay ahead for her. All she'd ever learnt about and wanted to know about was horses and she'd been living in a mobile home. She couldn't go back to either again. What on earth was going to happen? Each day, more and more questions flew around in her head. At no point during that time in the hospital did they tell her this is permanent. She always thought at some point she'd be walking again.

CHAPTER 28

That summer was really warm. Yvette came in and said, 'Gosh it's beautiful out there.'
Gabby said, 'Shall we just go out and look around?'
Yvette said, 'What about your physio?'
Gabby said, 'It's too nice to be stuck inside.'
So, they got ready and did a sneaky flit outside. They found that at the sports centre directly behind the hospital, they had the International Wheelchair Games on. This was something Yvette and Gabby found they really enjoyed watching. Whilst there, Gabby didn't feel so out of place, where most people were in wheelchairs.
In the evenings, Florence would come along and take Gabby down to the parties that were arranged for the athletes. Being in a wheelchair was like you had a pass to get through the door. They had many fun evenings down there. After 11pm, the hospital doors to the ward would be locked. Florence would push Gabby as fast as she could by running and it would be a race against time and night after night Gabby would be locked out.

The nurses would let them in and were not happy that Gabby was going out and coming back late, so they left her to sort herself out, getting undressed and ready for bed. Although with the nurses being annoyed, this became something that made Gabby become more independent.

In the hospital, as part of the rehabilitation, all patients were taught how to get in and out of a car. This was done with the physio and they had a car inside the hospital which had been cut apart to allow the patients to practice getting in and out and putting their wheelchair in with them. Gabby went along to her session and was really nervous. She didn't want to look silly but was not sure how she was ever going to get herself from a wheelchair into the car seat without falling.

She was told to put her feet on the floor to get some stability then to move forward on the chair. Then place one hand on the car seat and the other on the wheelchair seat, then lift herself across to the car. For new patients, this was a challenge. This was also a challenge Gabby was keen to master because she was told that when she could transfer in and out of a car by herself she could go on a weekend home. She wanted to do that so much. These were just visits but an incentive for trying as hard as they can to learn the new skills.

The bath transfers were horrible; they had to transfer in with shoes on to stop their feet from slipping. They were difficult as they had to have one hand on the side of the bath and the other on the wheelchair. Gabby found this the scariest of all of them. She would see the big gap between the chair and the bath and have visions of ending up on the floor.

At home, Gabby found that filling the bath first was better, putting both legs over the side of the bath, one hand on the chair and one hand on the bath, and lift. She would cover the side of the bath and the wheel with a towel to avoid damaging her skin. Then it was a big lift across. Having the water in the bath was an excellent help when transferring due to the buoyancy. She was more comfortable doing it in that way, but it was always a case of assessing the risks of what she was doing each day.

During this stage of her rehabilitation, she was in a different ward of the hospital where all patients went to when it was close to them leaving the spinal unit. Gabby was in a two-bed bay which she shared with a lady called Lara. She had also had a riding accident. She had been out hunting and her accident sounded horrific. She had a higher level of injury than Gabby so she had less sensation. They became good friends and would help each other out.

When it came to going to the physio, they had to work together at pushing each other to get through what they were doing. It got quite competitive. She already had a family and they would visit a lot. She also had lots of friends and one day whilst the two of them were on their beds, Gabby saw a familiar face; it was Suzanne Jenner. Gabby was super excited to see her walking in the ward and then she went to see Lara who was obviously a friend. Gabby was wondering if she'd recognise her at all but supposed not as when she met her all those years ago she had a riding hat on and now laying in a bed injured she had no reason to even consider she may have met her before. During her time next to Lara she got to see, though not speak to, a few riders who had adorned her bedroom walls over the years. It was like being next to a celebrity at times.

Learning each day was the normal thing to do whilst being in the spinal unit. Gabby was getting used to the routine and had made friends. She was more comfortable with the day-to-day physio sessions and occupational therapy she had to go through. It was a very strict place to be in but it was done to give all the patients the best chance of living as independently as possible when the time came to leave.

With all the activities going on, Gabby never had the chance to stop and think of the severity of what had happened. It hadn't sunk it and she was living day to day wanting to go home. She thought she'd be walking out of the hospital. Not one of the doctors actually told her this was how life was going to be from now on.

CHAPTER 29

Some nights in the hospital, it was like a party in Gabby's room; she had so many of her friends come to visit and a few came every day she was in. She also found it was a time when she would discover who her real friends were. All her friends from young farmers were so supportive and would be joking and messing about each visit and they never treated her any differently. This was something Gabby really held on to because not all people managed that.
Some of her friends couldn't cope; they stopped speaking to her and couldn't even look at her. She found that very hard. It was like the feeling of loss of a family member, but Gabby was grieving the loss of the use of her legs, a bit like they had died.
Whilst in the hospital, three of Gabby's friends, Owen, her ex-boyfriend, Dylan, Florence's ex-boyfriend and Harry, a farmer from the next village, were chatting to each other about raising money to buy her a wheelchair. They arranged to do a bale push to raise money. They had a round bale and pushed it for 25 miles.
They had a spare bale on a trailer in case the one they were pushing fell apart.

There was a parent driving behind with drinks. The day of the push it was on the radio. Gabby was so happy and so grateful with the thought of her friends doing this for her. She desperately wanted to go and watch part of it but the doctors wouldn't let her go. She had to be happy with just listening to their progress on the radio. One morning, Gabby was doing her physio and one of the nurses came in saying to her that she'd just had a delivery of a dozen red roses. She wanted her to go back straight away as they all were excited to find out who had sent them. So, Gabby went back to her room. The card on the flowers said 'All my Love' and she just assumed they were from the person she was riding for that day. She couldn't imagine she'd receive anything like that from anyone else. Later on that day, she had a phone call from Logan. He said he was on holiday and would visit when he got back. He asked if she'd been given lots of flowers and Gabby said yes, she had. She finished the call and then quickly realised the roses must have been sent by Logan. She phoned him straight back and asked if they were from him, he said yes. She felt so silly. She apologised for not realising. The closeness they had both shared during those college days continued and as friends they were close. It meant a lot to Gabby to have him there for her.

CHAPTER 30

After six long months in the hospital, she was finally allowed to go home. This was the day she'd been dreaming of but what if she couldn't cope? What if something happened and she didn't know what to do? It was a scary time. The hospital was very good and had a contact number she could call if she needed advice or any help. She also had a community nurse that would come to the house and check she was coping. This was reassuring, knowing they hadn't just wiped their hands of her.

Leaving the hospital and having to go back to living with her parents was when it finally hit her. Her life as it had been was ruined. She would no longer be able to ride her beloved Misty again and never be able to dance like she used to. That hurt her. How was she going to go out, have a life, work, have a family?

Gabby became very angry and frustrated. She took it out on Yvette and Yvette took all of the outbursts that Gabby was dishing out and never complained. She knew deep down this was not a personal attack. This was Gabby in distress and shock. Frightened of what might lay ahead.

Yvette said to Gabby one morning, 'Do you want to go to the shops and do some girl shopping?' Gabby really liked the idea of that and agreed to go. She thought it would be nice to get some new things. She was pushing herself along and felt people staring at her and didn't know how to cope with this. This hadn't been something she experienced in the hospital. This was a new feeling and it was not nice. She just looked down and didn't make any eye contact.

A friend of Yvette's came along and stopped to chat with her, so Gabby had to stop. She just sat listening to the conversation and the woman said to Yvette, 'How is she getting on?'

Gabby felt like screaming at her that she could hear her, why didn't she just ask her? This put Gabby in a foul mood and she just wanted to get back home and shut the door behind them and shut out all these people who would speak in a way that hurt her. How had she got to this? Life had been really good. Horses, friends, nights out, and now, nothing.

Life in a wheelchair was a serious shock to the system and she honestly wouldn't wish it on her worst enemy. As if things weren't bad enough with her not being able to walk, she also had the indignity of not having any control over her bladder and bowels. This was something nobody would know about unless they were involved.

Due to Gabby's mood, Walter asked her if she'd like to go and see the horses and have a sit on one of the ponies. She said she'd love to. She'd missed them. Missed the smell of them and being outside. Yvette helped her put on a body protector and Walter picked her up and onto Trigger and kept a good hold of her. Yvette took a photo and then Walter picked her up and put her back in her chair. She was horrified at the feelings she had when sitting on Trigger. She was petrified. She felt like her legs were being pulled out of the sockets. It was an awful feeling. She knew that day she would never get on a horse again.

CHAPTER 31

The first winter she was home after the accident it was very cold. As she was getting ready for bed, she noticed that she had a few black toes. She showed them to her mum and they both came to the conclusion that she'd somehow pinched them. So, they left it for a while. Then it got worse and it was obvious it wasn't just a pinch when all of her toes turned black.
They made an appointment and went to see the GP. He told her it was frostbite and that she was suffering from Raynaud's disease, which is hereditary. Yvette had it but Gabby had never suffered from it before and the doctor said the accident had brought it out. Yet more tablets and another worry.

Having that love for horses is an addiction. Just because she couldn't ride didn't mean she couldn't do other things. Gabby had a look at Horse Driving Trials and Showing. She decided showing was far too slow and boring.
Then she came across an advert for lessons with Lucy Spencer, a very well-known Horse Driving Trials competitor, who had represented Great Britain many times and won.

She was world champion when Gabby met her. Yvette rang her and told her about Gabby and because of Gabby being in a wheelchair, Lucy agreed to see her. She said that she could spend the day with her and at the end of the day, Lucy would tell them if she thought Gabby had what it takes to carry on in that sport.

That day was the start of a big change for Gabby. Lucy first took her out with a spotted pony and taught her the basics and gave her so much knowledge. It was so different from what she was used to and it felt very strange being so far away from the horse's head. They stopped for lunch where they went to a local pub and Walter asked Lucy if she thought Gabby would be good enough to compete. She said yes and that was the start of wonderful things.

After lunch, Gabby was allowed to drive a new horse in the yard that was very full of himself and she wasn't quite sure which one of them was in charge. Then the biggest moment and surprise of the day was when Lucy let her drive a pair of her Trakehners, 17.2hh each. They were amazing. She felt the strength of these animals and felt a happiness wash over her.

Lucy gave Gabby a lot in teaching her to drive horses, she treated her like any other student she had and they got around the balance situations and anything else that cropped up.

Gabby spent as much time as possible with Lucy trying to learn as much as she could and as she couldn't muck out, she cleaned the harnesses for her. It felt to her so nice to feel needed and of some use. She used to go in the tack room, take some lunch and lay out the harness on her lap. She would get covered in mud and smelled of wet leather and dirt, but to her, it was absolute heaven. Lucy gave Gabby her sanity back.

As time went by, Gabby spoke with her parents about getting a pony of her own to drive and they agreed. They were happy to help. She saw an advert in a paper and Gabby asked her friend to go and view the pony with her as she couldn't check an unknown pony out on her own in case she got kicked. The viewing went well and they decided to buy the pony that was called Thunder. He was a saint.

Yvette was her groom whilst on the carriage and Walter did all the carriage work, fixing, lifting and shifting. They took Thunder to Lucy's as often as possible. He was obviously learning too. When Gabby first started taking him to have lessons with Lucy, he was very green and they both had a lot to learn, but he showed promise and though a bit cheeky on the road, he seemed to know he had to look after her.

One day, they took him down to an outdoor school in Lucy's yard. They drove him down and Lucy got out to open the gate.

There was a huge puddle in between where she was and the gate that they needed to go through. That turned out to be their first obstacle. Thunder spooked and shied, attempting to drive up a tree trunk. Lucy picked Gabby up and put her on one of the jump fillers that were in the arena. She then took Thunder over a load of road cones which were laid on the ground for the purpose of running them over, to get him used to the noise. She did this over and over until he calmed down.

She then put Gabby back on the carriage to drive and they took him to a water jump on the grounds. They walked him in and out until he relaxed and after that day, he was ok to go through water. He still needed encouragement but he never shied away from it again.

Gabby started competing around the country and had written to lots of local companies asking for sponsorship to help her. One of the local wine bars did a special fundraising evening for her to raise money. She had a lot of support and some generous sponsors.

They continued to train and compete and it was just the medicine Gabby needed. She made a lot of friends and people were shocked to see a disabled person competing against able-bodied competitors.

Going up to check the leaderboard to see scores and seeing the looks on people's faces when they realised it was her that was up on the board amongst them was priceless. She made some really good friends.

Lucy gave her so many opportunities, including competing with two of her Trakehners in an indoor driving trial competition, and took her to events when she was going to do her demonstrations. She had the biggest heart and Gabby had so much love and respect for her.

CHAPTER 32

In between competitions, Gabby would continue
to see Lisa and one evening, Lisa called her and
said she was getting married and asked if Gabby
would be her bridesmaid. Gabby was over the
moon. She felt so happy to be asked. It was
something she said yes to straight away.
She had to go for dress fittings and Yvette went
along to them to help her in and out of dresses in
a confined space. They all had the giggles trying
to get the dresses on and not have to take parts
of their clothing off in the process. They
eventually decided on the dresses Lisa was
happy with and they all left to go and have a
cuppa close by and chat about the wedding
arrangements.
The wedding was to be held close to where Lisa
lived and then the reception would be in a hotel,
where they all would stay after. On the day of
the wedding, Gabby, Yvette and the other
bridesmaid were taken to the church first and
then they had to wait for the bride to arrive. On
reaching the church, they were faced with a
huge number of steps to the door which they
weren't expecting.

This was a slight concern but someone soon
came to the rescue and one of the men carried
Gabby up and Yvette took her chair and met
them at the top.

The wedding day was lovely; mainly close
family, and Gabby felt privileged to be involved
in Lisa's special day. There was lots of dancing
and Gabby and Yvette were totally worn out at
the end.

Before snuggling down for the night, they had to
get Lisa to come and get her clothes out of their
room as she had used it before the wedding to
get changed.

As they were walking to the room, the girls were
chatting and Lisa walked straight in front of
Gabby. As she did so, Gabby wheeled on the
wedding dress. Gabby shouted stop, just as Lisa
took another step and she heard a ripping
sound. Lisa had drunk quite a bit of wine that
evening and didn't even hear her. Gabby
managed to get off the dress and couldn't see the
damage. Lisa was so happy and excited and
never said a word about it. Even after the
wedding, the dress wasn't mentioned. And to
this day, Gabby still feels terrible when thinking
about it.

CHAPTER 33

Because of what happened on the day of the accident, Gabby had to go to court. She had to go to the High Court in London where she had to go before a judge and tell him what happened on that day. She was suing her boss, or one half of them, for leaving her paralysed. On the day of the accident, there were so many people on the ground but when it came to witnesses, nobody saw a thing. So, she only had two people speaking up for her. One was a polo player, Harry Ashton, and the other was her sister, Florence.

Gabby felt sick. It was sheer hell. She felt like a criminal in there. When she got to court, it turned out that her barrister knew her boss's dad through the army and they, along with the judge, were all known to each other. Gabby sensed things were not going to go well for her. Each day in court, they had to park in the car park at the side of the court, which was secure. And each evening leaving, they were met by lots of photographers trying to take photos of them leaving the court.

Gabby was driving and trying to get out and drive through London whilst being chased up the road was scary. Walter did his best to cover her with a newspaper but it wasn't easy with Gabby in the driving seat.

As the week came to an end, the judge ruled that it was just an accident. He also refused Gabby's right to appeal.

She didn't know what to do with herself. She just sat in court sobbing. All of those years. With such a horrific accident leading to her becoming wheelchair-bound, and then for the person who was responsible for her never to be walking again to walk out of court without blame was more than Gabby could comprehend. They were all patting each other on the back and celebrating and Gabby was in shock. She'd lost her trial and had no compensation for this most awful life-changing accident. This was something that would take her time to get her head around.

She couldn't understand how some people sailed through life and some had so much thrown at them like they were being punished. She went over and over it in her head. Was it something she did, or something she should have done? Was it because they were both so spoilt as girls that someone thought she needed a reality check? So many scenarios ran through her mind. Would she ever know why her?

CHAPTER 34

Other than competing, she started to go out to town in the evenings to meet people and try to make new friends. She would have an orange juice and play a game of pool or just watch the football. The friends she had coming into the hospital all had to get on with their lives and suddenly being at home and not seeing anyone was hard. She felt so lonely. She was used to being with her sister and they had been torn apart by this accident. It ruined her life and devastated Florence too.

She made a lot of friends with the soldiers in Wrenbridge, which was an army town, and the soldiers would be in town in the evenings and they were all very accepting. They invited her to parties and she'd go round to their houses and was even invited to weddings. There were also locals who were brilliant who she'd hang out with or go to the cinema with.

Gabby was going out and starting in one pub for an orange juice and chat with her friends and then would either go to another one with some of the friends or go alone to another and chat to people.

She realised one night that a man appeared to be following her. She thought perhaps he was doing the same pub to pub thing so she carried on with her night.

When she drove home that night she had a car close behind her. She looked in the mirror and could see what kind of car it was from the lights. It was something Gabby and Florence would do together, identifying cars by their lights. She drove into her driveway and then forgot about it.

The next time out, the same thing happened. The same man and the same thing on the way home. She told her parents and they said he was probably just going the same way. She was feeling a bit odd about it but as her parents said it had to be something explainable.

On the following weekend, she had a friend coming by who she met through some of her army friends. Richard lived about an hour away and was coming to take her out for the day. He arrived and Gabby decided to drive them both to where they were having lunch. It was great to meet up again. They had a good chat about the last time they had met and how everyone had such a great night. It was nice to see each other in daylight and talk about what they had both been up to since then.

Lunch was fun and as they were chatting and walking back to the car, she spotted the man who'd been following her before. She never said anything to Richard. They drove back towards her parents where he'd left his car and as she was driving, she saw the man in her mirror behind her. This time she told Richard about him. He told her to drive in then turn the car round, so she did.

They drove back out of her parents drive and the man had turned round to go back towards town, so she caught up with him. Richard wrote down his number plate and they overtook him to check it was definitely the same man. It was. They then went on a detour and went back to her parents from the opposite direction. She had to go as fast as possible to lose the man. When they got back to the house, Richard gave her the number. He said goodbye and thanked her for having lunch and they waved goodbye.

Gabby went in the house and told Walter what had happened. He got up straight away and said, 'Right, let's go to the police station.' So, off they went. Gabby was really scared going into a police station. She spoke to an officer who took the details down of what had been happening and she gave them the number plate she had with her written down. They told her not to worry and that they would look into it and give them a call when they had spoken to the man.

That evening, the phone rang and Walter answered it. They could tell he was speaking to the police.

Walter was listening and then said, 'Right, okay, I'll tell her, thank you.'

The call ended. He said the police had gone around to the man's house. He was in when they went and was very scared when they questioned why he had been following her. He admitted to following her and said that he just wanted to talk to her. The police told him to keep his distance and to stop with the following. The policeman said he thought she wouldn't have any more problems with this man as he looked petrified. Gabby wasn't followed by him again.

CHAPTER 35

That week, she concentrated on driving her pony as much as possible. Schooling him and practising her dressage tests. She also took him out on the road and across the bridle paths around them. Yvette and Gabby would have so many fun times driving across fields and taking in the scenery. They would do as much of it as possible away from traffic as Thunder was nervous on the road for anything bigger than a car. But whenever that happened, Yvette would jump off the carriage and hold onto his head to keep him still and happy. He wasn't a naughty pony; he was genuinely frightened and wanted to get as far away from the big vehicle as possible.

Something during his life must have really scared him and he found it hard to cope with but they helped him by being gentle with him and patient. He had a heart of gold and was a gentle little soul. He would not worry about Gabby going in his stable, she brushed him and picked out his feet, she put his harness on him and then he'd let her take him out of the stable where Walter would be waiting with the carriage.

The same would happen when they came back from exercise. He'd stand still whilst Gabby was put in her chair and then she'd unharness him and wash him off and put a sweat rug on him. He was as good as gold. He never pushed or shoved her and was the kindest little pony she could ever have. He was very special and they had so many happy times together.

One afternoon she took him out with Walter for a change. That was always a bit different because Walter was so much heavier on the carriage and was not quite as quick as getting out when needed like Yvette was. They were trotting along the road when they saw a lorry coming towards them quite fast. The lorry wasn't slowing down and was rattling and Gabby could feel the hesitation in Thunder. Walter just sat on the carriage and didn't get down, and the lorry continued to speed past. As he did, Thunder jumped sideways, tipping the carriage over. The carriage went upside down into the ditch. Walter fell off the side as it tipped and Gabby who was tied in the carriage was hanging upside down in the ditch. Thunder was also in the ditch, still attached to the carriage but standing still.

Suddenly lots of people appeared out of the houses they were next to.

A lady climbed into the ditch and took Thunder out of the carriage and walked him out of the ditch and then a man came and helped Walter get the carriage out after getting Gabby untied. She was then sat on a dining room chair in the middle of the road. The carriage was taken out of the ditch some way up the road. It was very deep and they had difficulty getting it out. The shafts on the carriage were bent and so they took it into the yard nearby and starting hammering it to straighten them out.

Thunder was shaken but didn't have a scratch on him and Gabby was given a very sugary cup of tea. It was amazing how quickly people rallied around to help them. Once the shafts were straight again they put Thunder back to and Walter picked up Gabby and put her back in the carriage. They thanked all the people that had helped them and then drove back to the stables. Thunder was a little nervous on the drive back but considering what had happened he was coping remarkably well. After getting Thunder comfortable and making sure the other horses were in clean beds, fed and watered they went back to the house. They sat and told Yvette about what had happened. She was shocked but glad there was no lasting damage to Thunder or either of them.

It was definitely a day that taught them Walter wasn't agile enough to be sitting next to Gabby when she needed someone by Thunder's head reassuring him.

CHAPTER 36

One weekend, there was a wheelchair basketball
game at the same town where the spinal unit
was. Gabby went along to watch with her
cousin, Molly. They watched the game and then
walked back to the car. Whilst they were
chatting about the game they both noticed
Gabby had something under her windscreen
wiper and for a moment they thought it was a
parking ticket, but it wasn't.
It was a card that said 'Not sure if you remember
me from college but it would be nice to meet up
sometime.'
It had the lad's name and number on the card.
She didn't recognise the name and it was strange
but exciting at the same time. The girls laughed
about it on the drive back trying to think who it
could have been who left the note and they
wondered if that person was watching the
basketball with them.
Gabby left it for a while before contacting the
person on the card but she was curious to see
who it was. She arranged to meet him in the
wine bar where they did the fundraising.

They agreed to keep an eye on her in case it was a dangerous person and she needed help getting away. The meeting was fine though. They got on well, even though she didn't recognise him at all. He worked in agriculture and so they did have a lot in common to chat about.

After that, Gabby decided to invite him to the Polo ball. He came and they had fun but she wasn't sure how things would go with them. She still felt that being close to someone and not having the ability to walk away made her feel vulnerable, so she was cautious about where she went and who she went out with.

She had a call from him one day saying his parents wanted to know if she could have children. Gabby looked at her mum who was trying her best to hear what was being said. She could tell Gabby was not happy about something. She had only been seeing this person for a few weeks and for him to ask her about babies freaked her out. She decided that day that he wasn't who she wanted to be with. She had to get used to being in a chair and having someone ask that kind of question wasn't something she was ready to even think about at that time.

CHAPTER 37

That weekend, she had a competition to focus on and it was a long way from home so Yvette and Gabby had to sleep in a tent and Walter slept in the Luton in the lorry and Thunder was in the back. It was a lovely big course and the hazards were quite technical but Gabby was happy to be able to put all her practise into the real thing. The dressage test went well despite the continual rain. They had to go back to the lorry and get ready for the cross-country phase. As they were walking back, there was an announcement on the Tannoy saying a helicopter was about to land. They said to hold on to the horses and ensure you help anyone if they needed the extra help. Gabby was shocked at this and very worried, especially as Thunder wasn't happy with things on the road, let alone a helicopter coming in to land from the sky. She had visions of them careering round the countryside.

Seconds later, the helicopter arrived. Thunder was joined by people who held onto both sides of his head reassuring him and he stood still and wasn't too upset by the strange monster from the sky.

When it took off again and left, they made a huge fuss of Thunder telling him how good he was and praising him, and also praying they never have to experience that again. A young driver had broken her leg and was going to be okay, but she had to stay in the hospital for the night as she had bumped her head when she fell from her carriage.

CHAPTER 38

Back at home, Gabby decided to go out one night and chatted to people she knew when there was live music on in the wine bar. She also made some friends there. The singer, Dean's, girlfriend, Lily, became a friend and she'd sit and chat with her and her friends. They were fun to be around and she had a lot of laughs. Especially with Quinn, who was Lily's brother. She was in the pub with the group of them one night and they invited her to join them for Chinese. She had eaten but said she'd go to chat. They introduced her to a band and to the owner of a recording studio. Gabby had no idea there was such a thing in Wrenbridge. This was really exciting for her to speak to these people. They asked her to go to the studio with them after they had finished eating to see what they were doing. She went along and was given a little tour whilst being carried around by the singer, who happily picked her up and walked around with her. She went to the studio a lot to listen to the recording and she also went along to a music festival in a park with the group of friends.

She felt so happy to have a group of friends who invited her to places despite the chair, which was always the "elephant in the room" in Gabby's mind. That was the thing though, it didn't occur to them.

Quinn told her, 'Before you had the accident, you were a wonderful girl and after, you are a wonderful girl that struggles with stairs.' Hearing that really meant a lot to her. She was her own worst enemy for thinking how other people may see her.

A few months later, Gabby went into Wrenbridge as normal and bumped into Dylan, an ex-boyfriend's brother. They had a good catch up and with Gabby not working, she offered him a lift home. He was happy to accept and they both set off towards Gabby's car.

As they were walking and talking, Gabby became aware that there were four men behind following them. She told Dylan and he told her to ignore them and keep going. They got to the car and as she transferred in they caught up. They threw her chair across the path and started punching her in the back of her head. She was trying desperately to hang on to the steering wheel and not get dragged out of the car. She really thought they were going to kill them both. The men were slamming Dylan's leg in the car door and it was bleeding.

Gabby had her hand on the car horn to try to get help but the people walking past didn't stop. They were being watched however by someone living above a shop and they phoned the police. When the police arrived, the men ran off. Gabby then shouted at Dylan thinking it was his fault and told him to find his own way home. She was in floods of tears and the police waited with her until she calmed down and followed her home to take a statement.

Arriving at her parent's house with the police was a fright for Yvette and Walter. They both had to sit and listen to what had happened. The police were amazing; by the next morning all four men had been caught. They were all charged and it went to court. Gabby was told that she wasn't allowed to attend because seeing her would influence the judge's decision. All the men got community service. They were told they were not allowed near Gabby or they would be arrested straight away.

This incident had frightened Gabby so much that she began having panic attacks. She was too scared to go out and would stay in the house and read or watch the television. She did have counselling and chats to victim support to help her get over it but it was just something else that she had to deal with.

CHAPTER 39

Trying to move on from this latest ordeal, she thought she'd start looking at what she could do next. She enrolled in a computer course as she had no option than get herself an office job. She passed her exam and started to look for jobs. She spoke to a friend who lived in the same village who worked in an oil company, Keenan Oils, and she said they were looking at taking someone else on. She got an interview and was offered the job. She took the job and found that she really enjoyed it. She learned so much and there were so many happy times there. There was always so much going on. It was always very busy but it kept them all going and time went flying by. All the customers became recognisable on the phone and in person when they would come to pay.

Molly got married that year and Gabby went along to the wedding and met a man called Ross who was playing the bagpipes at the wedding. He was from Canada and said she should pay him a visit.

So, after a while, Gabby decided to save up and make her first holiday after her accident a trip to Canada. She eventually booked herself a two-week holiday to meet up with Ross, who was going to show her the sights.
It was a scary prospect but she wanted to do this and thought it would do her good to feel that, yes she can do this. So, she saved up and booked to go over on a holiday.

She got to Canada and found that Ross wasn't there to meet her. This wasn't a great start but not to be put off, she flagged down a taxi and he took her to the motel she was staying at for the holiday. She got settled into the little room she was staying in which had a bed, a set of drawers and a small bathroom. It was basic but comfortable and clean. Gabby went into the restaurant joined to the motel and found out details of how to get into the town and details on excursions she could go on.
The whole time Gabby was in Canada, she didn't hear a word from Ross. This didn't put her off. She went into the town and it was beautiful. So, she went and booked to go whale watching and other sightseeing trips. The day she went whale watching, the captain of the boat came over and asked her if she was on her own and would she like him to show her around.

She said yes as she was alone and that it would
be lovely. His name was Connor and he took her
all over. They went to different places to eat,
parks, the citadel, and they also went to a Blues
Bar most evenings to eat, listen to live music,
and she met some of his friends.

They got really close when she was there and by
the time she was due to go home she didn't want
to leave. They went to a department to see if she
could stay over there but it wasn't as easy as
that.

The day she was going home, she'd spent the
night worrying about leaving and not wanting
to leave Connor. She put the television on and
what she saw was something that to start with
made her think it was a film. A plane was flying
straight into two towering buildings. She quickly
realised that this was actually the news she was
watching and that what she was seeing was
happening as she watched. It was horrific. The
sight was something that would stay with
everyone who watched that morning for the rest
of their lives and even more so for those who
were involved or their friends and relations.

The next minute, there was a knock on Gabby's
motel room door. She answered it and it was the
lady from the restaurant to tell her the plane she
is supposed to be on was cancelled due to the
terrorist attack.

Gabby thanked her for letting her know and quickly tried to call her parents. The phone wouldn't work and she didn't know what to do about it. She needed to let them know that she wasn't going to be at home when they were expecting her.

She managed to get into town and met up with Connor to use a phone and try to get through from there.

She finally got through to them and told them she wasn't able to get back yet. That she was fine and that she'd let them know what was happening but could they please contact the travel agent to try to help her come home on a different flight.

After she had spoken to them, she had to go back to the motel and wait until the travel agent called to let her know what flight was going to take her home. She was really scared. She didn't want to go home in the first place but even more so after seeing the events on the news. All she could do was keep the television on and stay in her room. She was very lucky that the motel owners were letting her stay on free as she had been on a tight budget and she had no money left.

A couple of days after the planes crashing, she was sat in her room and the lady from the restaurant came by again to let her know they had just announced the plane going back to London was going to be leaving soon. She didn't want to go without seeing Connor first. She rang and he got a taxi over. The restaurant owner and her cousin offered to take her to the airport and they took Connor with them too. The ladies bought her some flowers. They were wonderful ladies who had been so kind to her whilst she was there.

It wasn't a long journey to the airport but the security was really tight and slow. Literally everything was checked. Gabby had bought her dad a penknife which was in her suitcase. This had to be taken out. She had to give it to the airport staff to throw away as it was something that could be used as a weapon.

Whilst they were all having their luggage checked, the police went into the ladies' toilet. Gabby had tried going in but the police told her to wait. When they came out, they had a woman who had a gun and they had arrested her. How someone could do such a thing, especially with what had happened with the towers was beyond belief.

That holiday did Gabby good in proving to herself she could still look after herself and have fun independently.

She was quite unhappy for a while after that holiday. She missed Connor. They kept in touch but since then, they hadn't ever managed to meet up again.

She went back to work and had lots of stories to tell of her trip away. After a couple of days, it felt like she hadn't been away. People still ran out of oil every day, people rang and wanted a chat as well as an order, and there were always fun conversations between the drivers and office staff.

CHAPTER 40

During this time, Florence had met someone and got married. Gabby was so happy for her and was excited to be able to help with organising the wedding with her. They had a lot of fun together shopping for the things Florence needed and Gabby was out and about making sure it all came together on the day. When they were married, it made Gabby feel a bit lost. Her other half had been joined to someone else and it was hard to not think that he had taken Florence away from her and not get caught up feeling annoyed.

She didn't do that though and when Florence announced they were expecting a baby, Gabby was thrilled for them. They had a beautiful baby boy, followed a couple of years later by another little boy. Gabby loved the boys so much; it was such a great job being an Aunty.

Gabby was very much the proud Aunt. She would go over and babysit as often as possible. Florence and her husband wanted to see Gabby with her own partner, so they set her up on a blind date. Gabby was okay with it. A bit nervous, but thought it was worth going along.

She met the blind date whose name was Troy in a pub in Wrenbridge. He was really good looking, funny and easy to talk to. She was blown away with how he made her feel. Troy was her first proper boyfriend since her accident. He competed in kickboxing and she would go to see him compete; he was very good. It was really exciting to watch and she was really proud to be with him. She was so happy being with him. She hadn't dated anyone she trusted and felt safe with until Troy. He showed her that she could still do a lot of things and be happy with someone and make them happy too.
Each day she saw him, she felt her heart skip a beat. He took her out for dinner one night to a lovely restaurant. This was the first time she'd ever been taken to dinner by a man. Even before the accident she had never been to dinner with a man. It was a special evening. They sat in a beautiful restaurant together and Gabby felt so grown up. She looked at the menu and picked something simple; she didn't want to be dropping food all over her or getting sauce on her face.
They chatted easily during dinner and Troy's hand reached over and took Gabby's, his thumb rubbing her hand as they talked. A warm feeling inside her made her feel like she was glowing with happiness.

She couldn't believe this person was with her and was treating her so well. He never knew her walking but treated her with such respect and gentleness.

They went out one night and ended up staying at one of Troy's friend's houses. They got to the house and Troy needed to get the door open. It was so dark and he couldn't see to put the key in the door, so he picked Gabby up, then sat her on a wheelie bin next to do the door whilst he got the door open, and then took her in his arms and carried her in.

They saw a lot of each other and as each day passed, Gabby realised she was falling for him. He made her forget all the events in the past and gave her hope. He was very loving and caring. He worked in the building trade and was busy. On some days, Gabby would take food to him to where he was working.

They would meet up most nights and spend as much time together as possible. Troy suggested going away on a weekend. So, they booked up and went away, not far away but far enough to be in new surroundings and have a little break together. They drove together and chatted about what they'd been doing. When they got to the hotel, they checked in and went to see their room.

It was lovely, a big bed, huge window looking out onto fields and the bathroom was all accessible which was just what Gabby needed to help her relax.

They dumped their bags on the floor and stopped and looked at each other. This was the first time they had been together where they were totally alone. Troy stepped forward and kissed Gabby softly to start with but then with passion. She was dizzy with emotion and wanted to be swept up by the wave. He took her in his arms off the chair and onto the bed. They lay together on the bed and continued kissing and touching. They knew they had to get to a dinner reservation but both of them didn't want to stop. They wanted each other fully at that moment. They didn't stop; Troy removed her clothes, telling her how beautiful she was. She did the same with his and they slowly made love to each other.

The connection between them was a heady mix. Gabby felt drunk but had not had a spot of alcohol. That night they showered and went to dinner. They were late for the reservation but it wasn't busy and they got a table straight away. They sat on a table for two and held hands across the table whilst chatting. They ordered their food and ate in companionable silence.

They finished eating and were drinking and chatting about the following weekend where Troy would be kick-boxing and he wanted her to come and watch him. Gabby was scared of the thought of someone hurting him but really wanted to go and support him. She was also really happy that he was happy to be seen out with her.

They went back to their room and back to bed. They lay together, skin on skin. Kissing and touching and exploring each other's bodies. Happiness was what she was feeling. And she wanted it to last forever.

The following weekend, they got ready for a kickboxing competition Troy was taking part in. They arrived in the town after about an hour drive. Gabby was proud to be going along to see Troy fight. They parked up and went into the venue.

Gabby stayed with some of Troy's friends whilst he got ready. He came out ready to go in the ring. It was a horrible feeling to start with. Gabby felt like grabbing him out of the ring and punching the other bloke but as she sat and watched, she soon realised Troy was good, really good, and this was exciting to watch. She was soon shouting at him to hit him. He won that competition and Gabby was so proud of him. She sat with him and watched the other people boxing after him.

There were some children doing it and Gabby was shocked to see them taking part at a young age.

Troy said, 'They could be ours one day.'

Gabby always remembered that comment. And the thought was something she would still think of many years after.

For no reason, they started drifting back into normal daily life and didn't see so much of each other. It wasn't something they discussed and Gabby never knew if this was a conscious decision or if they were just busy and the timing wasn't right. She did know however that he was her first true love. She would never forget their time together.

CHAPTER 41

Gabby continued to work at the oil company
and also to go out in the evenings but she also
joined a gym. Some of her friends were opening
a new gym in Wrenbridge and they asked for
her input on what they could do to make it
accessible for everyone. She helped them out
and in return, they allowed her discounted
membership.

It was totally amazing to get a trainer to show
her around the machines and work out a routine
for her to do to focus on the parts she needed to
tone up. Gabby started going three times a week
after work. She felt her confidence rise and her
body was looking better and getting stronger
each day.

After joining the gym, she had a lot of friends
who were always going out. She'd do her gym
session on a Friday after work, go home, have a
shower and then go back into town for the
evening.

She was having a drink, dancing with her
friends and she met a man who was standing
and watching the dancing. He was called Jakub;
he was Polish.

He seemed like a lovely lad and she found out he worked for a well-known film director. She arranged to go out on a date with him and they got on well. He was quiet and polite and she found all the stories he had to tell were so interesting.

She was learning a lot about his different culture and he also introduced her to listening to classical music. He wanted to know everything she did each day and who she spoke to and what they said and what she said. It was a strange way to live. She would go about her day, hoping she didn't say the wrong thing to cause more problems. He didn't have to shout, she knew when things were wrong by the tone of his voice or by what he said to her.

One night, she had a shock coming. Jakub came in the room and wanted to know what she was doing. She told him she was getting ready for the next day.

He said, 'Why do you need to do this now? Is something special going on? What haven't you told me?'

She felt sick. She said it was just to save time in the morning. She wanted to be more productive. He didn't believe her. He said, 'Where are you going?'

She said, 'Nowhere.'

He wanted to know who she was going to see or speak to when she was out, was she going to try to impress someone? She was freaking out inside. As much as she said it was just going into town, that she didn't speak to anyone and came straight home, he just didn't believe her.

She said she wouldn't get her stuff out then, that it didn't matter that her clothes weren't out. She shoved them back in the cupboard.

As she did this, he flipped, shouting at her for now going back on what she was doing. She was at a loss for what to do now.

The tears started to flow; she had no way of stopping them.

This made him angrier, saying, 'Here we go. Here come the waterworks.'

What she wanted to do was run away. She wanted to grab her stuff and run and keep running. But she couldn't get out of the house on her own.

She resigned to the fact that this was how she'd made her bed and she'd have to lay in it.

The days went by and she was careful how she spoke and how she acted and behaved.

She went on with each day, treading on eggshells and waiting for the next explosion as there was always one brewing.

That came one night after he came in after being at the pub.

He had been out drinking with friends and wasn't happy about her still being at his home, knowing fully well that he was the one that left her there when he went out. He knew with her being in his house she couldn't go anywhere. He wanted to know what she'd been doing and why was she wide awake. She said she was just watching the TV and reading.

He said, 'Has someone been here?'

She said, 'Like who?'

Which turned out to be a big mistake. He slapped her hard across the face. She shrank back clutching her face.

He said, 'Now look what you made me do. That was your fault. Why do you make me do that?'

She didn't want to speak and just sat on the bed, tears pricking her eyes. She just wanted him to stop talking and let her out of the house. He was not about to stop now though. He wanted to know why she wasn't answering him.

Christmas came and Jakub said they had both been invited to his employers for Christmas Eve. Gabby was really excited, she had never met anyone in the film industry before. She got dressed up and met Jakub at his house and both of them went to the big house. They were taken in and were made to feel so welcome. They gave them both gifts and showed Gabby what they had been working on in the latest bout of filming.

They went back to the house and the following day, Gabby picked up Jakub and took him home as her parents had said he could come for Christmas day. Gabby was desperately hoping he didn't fly off the handle whilst there.

When they were there, he asked to use Gabby's computer and she realised he sat talking to girls in chat rooms. She was not happy and he was acting strangely.

At the end of the day, she drove him back to his house. He said she could come in for a while so he carried her into the house and said he wouldn't bring her chair in this time. Alarm bells should have been ringing but she didn't realise what was about to happen.

She was sat in an arm-chair and Jakub climbed on her and knelt on her arms. She couldn't move and she told him he was hurting her. He didn't say a word. He then put his hands around her throat, he was pressing hard and Gabby started struggling to get free, she was wriggling and finally managed to get an arm free and shoved him away from her.

She screamed at him to take her to her car and prayed he wouldn't refuse. Thankfully, he didn't. As soon as she was in her driving seat, she slammed the door and locked it. She drove away and never went back.

She told her mum what happened that night but didn't mention it to her dad because she knew he would have wanted to kill him.

On a summer day Gabby had gone in to town and met a new friend, Amy who had asked her to join her at a different pub than she was used to going to. She was happy to try it out, she drove her new friend and herself to this pub and as they both went in it was obvious that Amy was well known there. It was a warm day so they got a drink and went outside to sit down. They were soon surrounded by people. Some of them Gabby knew from school and some were new to her. She was enjoying the new surroundings and there was a lot of laughter. Gabby met Amy's brother Danny that day too. He had just been released from prison. To Gabby it didn't matter, she was not aware what the reason was but they were nice to her so she thought nothing of it. Amy invited Gabby round to her house after work on days that Gabby wasn't going to the gym. She would go there and have tea with them. Amy would get out all her moisturiser's and they'd go through them together, looking at the new brands and trying them all. It was fun being at Amy's house. She and Danny were both so nice and they watched television with their dinner on their laps. Whilst she was there they would have lots of people coming by. Gabby sometimes saw the people but a lot of the time they would just go to answer the door, disappear upstairs and then go back to sit down with Gabby after they'd left.

They spent lots of time going out, to the pub or the cinema and then going back to Amy's after. They were a new crowd of people but they welcomed her with open arms.

Whilst Gabby was at work one afternoon she saw her Dad drive in. She asked her boss if it was ok to go and see what he wanted and he said yes. She pushed out of the door and Walter had a newspaper on his lap. She went over to the car door and he said, "Is this who you've been hanging out with"? She looked at the newspaper and on the front page was Amy and Danny. The article said that they both had been arrested for drug dealing. Things suddenly made more sense why all the people had been coming by the house and going upstairs. Gabby had been totally naïve and not realised this was what was happening. All the time she'd been in the house with them, her car was outside which had her name all over it from the sponsorship for the Horse Driving Trials. And during that time the police had been outside watching the house. She had no idea and felt gutted that these people she had trusted turned out to be dealing drugs. Walter was cross with her but she had no idea what had been going on. She had never seen any drugs in the house and if she had she'd have never gone back in there. She was just relieved the police hadn't thought she knew anything.

Each weekend Gabby would go to town and spend the evening dancing in the only pub in town with a dance floor. She'd dance with her friend Selina who would whisk her around the room. They had such a great time. The atmosphere was brilliant in there. She felt normal being in there with her friends. She forgot about the chair, all the people she was with would dance with her and have a laugh. She tried to get back to the car before the pubs shut because she didn't want to get caught up with drunks walking home. Most evenings she'd give her soldier friends lifts back to the barracks as it was on her way home. She was used to it, she'd drive up to the camp. They would check who was in the car, she'd drop off the person who she'd given the lift too. Then she'd turn round and drive back out of the camp. She'd then go home.

One weekend she was going back and a lad she'd seen talking to some people she knew asked her for a lift. She didn't know him but she said she'd give him a lift. He told her where to take him and he chatted to her on the way to his house. All was fine. She dropped him off and then went home. She found out the following day the person who she'd picked up had just been released from prison where he'd been charged for murder.

This came as a bit of a shock but Gabby said, he hadn't done anything to her and he'd obviously done his time so who was she to say he was now a bad person. Her naivety was showing through again. The following weekend she again went to the same pub and stayed till closing time, she pushed back to the car. Her friends she'd been dancing with walked back to the car with her and she started to drive home. That night she was driving off the pedestrian area with her car window open. A man came over and said to her, "Which way are you driving"? Gabby told him where she lived and he said, "Oh you go past my house, can I hitch a lift"? She said, yes of course and he moved her chair into the boot and she started driving. He was a bit older than her but was dressed nice and looked respectable. He asked her to drive left to where he lived and she went along the road. He told her a few lefts and rights and then he suddenly asked her to stop the car.

She was in the middle of nowhere. She was trying not to panic. He said he just needed to sit still for a minute. She sat in the car and said to him that she needed to go home and please would he get out.

This was when he said "No". Alarms started going off. She was stupid, what had possessed her to pick up a total stranger and drive to the middle of nowhere and then stop.

She hadn't told anyone where she was and she had no idea who this person was. How was she going to get him out of the car? Her chair was in the boot so she was stuck. She sat there for a moment and he started phoning people. His phone also rang at one point and he was shouting at the person on the end, which Gabby soon discovered was his girlfriend. She listened to the conversation and then said, "Please get out, I need to get going". He said, "If you don't want me in here, take me to North Lane housing estate. She turned the car on and drove, he didn't tell her which house, he just told her to stop the car again. This time she was in a built up area. He got out the car and she didn't even wait for him to put the chair in the front. She locked the doors and drove off. She'd learnt a huge lesson that night. Anything could have happened. She never told her parents what she'd done. They would have been horrified.

The next day was a Sunday and Gabby went shopping with Yvette to a large shopping centre about an hour away from home.
They both loved shopping together and could spend all day browsing around all the shops. They parked the car and went in. As they were going past a book shop they noticed a celebrity weather girl doing book signings.

Gabby loved books so was keen to go and get one and have it signed. So they both went into the shop. They got a book and sat in the queue. When it came to her turn she went to the table, handed the lady her book and told her what she wanted written in it.

The lady had a brief chat with Gabby and Yvette and then they turned to go to the till to pay for the book. Yvette was in front and Gabby was following. She was busy making her way when she heard the lady shouting for her to stop. Gabby stopped straight away and as she looked towards the celebrity author she saw the table cloth on the table was tangled in her wheels. The lady was hanging on to the books on the table and the big vase of flowers. The police who were in the shop for the lady's security were laughing and so were all the other people queuing. Gabby was mortified. She reversed her chair up to release the table cloth and then went to pay. She thought, that was definitely one way to get a celebrity to remember you. Yvette and Gabby paid for the book and as soon as they were out of the shop, they looked at each other and laughed their heads off.

CHAPTER 42

Back at work, they had lots of deliveries every
week and on some occasions, Gabby was
allowed in the lorry with the drivers. She loved
it. She went one day to deliver fuel to where a
band she loved was playing at a music festival,
in the hope of seeing them. She didn't have her
chair with her so she had to rely on her driver
colleagues to show her if anything good was
happening when they got there. They pulled up
to the field and the driver got waved in by the
security and as they made their way to the oil
tank, Gabby heard the band she was hoping to
see. They were on stage doing a sound check.
She looked at the driver and said to him, 'Please
can we stop, just a minute?' He said, 'Oh ok, just
a quick one,' and they sat, watched and listened.
She was also lucky enough to go to the British
Grand Prix for the weekends. She'd go with the
driver in a lorry to deliver fuel and see the
drivers practicing during the beginning of the
weekend. She'd then get her car and drive to the
circuit and had a pass to stay all weekend.
She would sleep in the car and go to the party
the night before the race that they held there.

It was something she really enjoyed and she managed it every year. She was most happy when she got to see her favourite Ferrari driver. The drivers felt like older brothers to her and she chatted to them about most things and they also liked teasing her about stuff too, but her work colleagues and bosses were also a bit like family.

Life had dealt Gabby so many dramas in her life. She felt her confidence was decreasing again. Deciding to not go out for a while again, she went online to chat rooms to speak to people but not be near them. She chatted to people with the same interests and she regularly talked to people in the UK and Canada.

She met a man that lived on a small island near England. It was a British Island. She found he was easy to chat to and she told him everything. It was good to talk to someone who had no idea who she was and didn't have any thoughts of what she had been like before. When she was at work Gabby couldn't wait to get home and start chatting to him again. His name was Carl and he was a couple of years older than her. He was into motorsports. He raced motorbikes and he loved music and playing in bands. They talked every day and he asked if she wanted to come over for New Year's Eve.

When Gabby mentioned this to her mum, she was not happy. She was scared Gabby would be going off to a strange place to meet someone who could be an axe murderer but Gabby was adamant that all would be well and Yvette agreed, albeit reluctantly.

On the day they were meeting, Gabby went through the arrivals hall and as the door opened, there was Carl waiting for her with a rose and he was filming the meeting. It was a strange sensation meeting someone you knew so much about but hadn't met in person but they both felt like they were friends already.

He helped her with her luggage and they went outside to his car. He had a lovely old red Porsche, Gabby got into the car and Carl was taking her chair apart to put in the car. As he put the frame in the car, it got caught on the roof of the car and tore the material inside. Gabby was mortified and offered to pay for it but he wasn't annoyed.

They drove to where he lived in a house he shared where they were going to be having a takeaway with his housemates that evening. They had a great evening. Lots of alcohol was consumed and there were lots of laughs. Carl's housemates were some of the loveliest people you could meet. And also, the funniest.

The following day, New Year's Day, Carl's mum had invited them for a dinner.

Carl's aunt and uncle were staying there too and Gabby was really nervous. She asked Carl if they could find somewhere nearby to use the toilet before they got there. He pulled up to some toilets and carried her in. He said he'd wait outside the door and call his mum to let her know they would be there shortly.

As he went outside, he shut the door and as the door shut, it locked. Gabby had the key and no chair so she had no way of reaching the door. She tried throwing the key out of the small window but it hit the edge and pinged off to the other side of the toilet onto the floor. She was stuck. Carl had to force the lock to get her out. Eventually, he got her out but Gabby was shaking with cold and nerves. He found it funny that she mentioned being scared and was not about to let her forget that incident.

The next day, it was time for Gabby to go home. She spent the last few hours having a tour of the island. It was a pretty island but very small and remote. Being surrounded by sea was something that scared her; she was much more comfortable with fields and countryside for miles.

CHAPTER 43

They continued to see each other. Carl would travel to England and Gabby would go to see him. They decided to find a place together and Carl was on the hunt for a place with room for her chair to get round. At that time, Gabby handed her notice in and had a month to work. Carl found a big apartment and it had two double bedrooms, both with ensuites, and their room had an enormous walk-in wardrobe area. It was perfect for them.

Saying goodbye to her parents was hard but equally difficult and, in some ways more so, was saying goodbye to her animals. Gabby gave up all her horses, her dog, and cat to be with Carl. She also left all her friends that day.

An emotional journey to the harbour was the start of new things. Gabby had to enrol in job agencies to find work. It was very scary because she had no experience in banking or law firms so she had to be prepared to try anything. She started temping for a bank and learnt a lot. She would have been happy to have a permanent job with them but they only had temporary work at that time. She then found her first full-time permanent job.

She was a newbie but learnt a lot and found it interesting. She quickly came to realise that there was a huge difference in the people she worked with and herself. She was doing the job for the money at the end of the month. All her colleagues were fiercely career-minded. She stayed there for a few years but it wasn't a happy place to work. There was a lot of bitching and back stabbing and Gabby hated it. She didn't want to be working like this every day.

Their days revolved around going to work and then the evenings were spent going to Carl's band practice, which was most nights at that time. He also did sprints and hill climbs with his motorbikes on weekends so she'd be taking photos and video, or just being there for support. Life continued like this for a couple of years. Whilst they lived in town she would just push to work as parking was not easy. Plus this kept up her fitness as she could no longer afford to go to a gym living away from England as it was too expensive.

Carl would take part in hill climbs on his motorbike. It was usually on a bank holiday and they'd get up really early. The car would be loaded up with tyre warmers, all the tools for the bike, fuel and leathers.

Carl had put a rack on the back of Gabby's car
that he could lift the bike on so they could travel
with it on like that and get to the hill on time.
With Carl competing he sometimes needed
someone to marshal for him and many times
Gabby would help out for the day to help with
Carls points. She mostly was on the radio to let
the people in the commentary box know when
the next bike was coming up the hill and also
letting those know at the bottom of the hill what
was going on and when the bike that had just
left them reached the finish post. It was a long
day. Gabby would be sat at the top of the hill all
day. She could only have a toilet break when it
was lunch time as she couldn't get in them
without help.

On other hill climbs she'd stay at the bottom to
just take photos at the start line and found this
better but it was still a long day. It always
seemed to her that no matter what day it was, it
always felt cold down that hill. The wind from
the bay came off the sea and made if feel quite
chilly. Gabby had gone down to where the bike
had been parked and Carl had gone to do his
next run up the hill. She wrapped herself in the
tyre warmers to keep warm whilst he was gone.
She heard to commentary start and heard Carl
had started. Then she heard a loud, "Oh no, Carl
is down".

She felt sick. What had happened? She couldn't get up the hill.

Was he on his feet? Did he need to go to the hospital? So many things went through her mind.

One of Carl's friends came over to her and said, "Don't worry, he'll be ok, he's back on his feet". He gave her a hug and stayed with her until they saw him coming towards them. He'd hit a slippery corner and the bike went out from under him. He had some messed up leathers but no broken bones and no need for hospital. His helmet was also badly damaged but it had done its job.

They packed up the car when Carl got back as he was too sore to continue. They got back in the car and they had help with putting the bike on the car to save Carl from having to lift it. Luckily this was the only incident they had to cope with of that kind but it was always something that scared Gabby at every competition after it.

CHAPTER 44

One month, Carl went to Singapore for work. Gabby was going to be at home alone and was not really looking forward to it. She was okay during the day as she had work but she was a bit scared about being in the apartment on her own. One of Carl's band friends and his wife invited Gabby for a dinner on one of the nights. She managed to find the house after some driving around. For Gabby getting round the Island was a nightmare; she got lost wherever she went. She had a nice time that evening, had dinner and the couple had some lovely cats she got to play with for a while. She didn't want to stay late in case she got lost on the way back. She said thank you and her goodbyes and set off back to the apartment. She was feeling okay about the journey; she'd double checked it when she got in the car. She'd written it down and had it stuck to her dashboard. She was happily driving along when she spotted police check ahead.

She stopped the car and the policeman came to the window and asked her where she had been and where she was going.

She told him and started feeling very scared. He checked around her car and when he got to the front he stopped by where the tax disc goes. He did some writing and then came back to the window.

He said, 'Your insurance is out of date.'

Gabby burst into tears. She said, 'I do have it. I didn't realise you had to put it in the window.'

He said, 'You're not in England now.'

He wrote on a piece of paper and handed it to her saying she had to go to a Parish hall inquiry the following week and have proof of her insurance. On the Island, they have different kinds of police and different rules and this was one of them. This scared her; she cried all the way back to the apartment.

She tried contacting Carl that night when she was in bed, terrified that she was going to be charged for something. When she told Carl, he said not to worry, to just make sure she had it, which she had already made sure of before phoning him. It was in the file box. Why were the rules all different here?

That Christmas was spent at Carl's parent's house. His brother and his girlfriend were also there.

They all swapped presents and Carl bought Gabby a fishing rod. Gabby was thinking what a nice present, but had not been fishing before. She was also a bit surprised by it.

They drove to Freda and Les's house; Carl's parents. It was totally different to spending Christmas with her own family. Again, they were swapping presents and chatting. Freda was doing the cooking and Les was carrying around drinks to everyone. Gabby and Carl were staying at his parents' that night so they could both have a drink. Carl walked off into the bedroom and Gabby was chatting to Oscar's (Carl's brother's) girlfriend.

When Carl came out, he said there is one more present and walked over to Gabby. He went down on one knee and asked her to marry him. Freda nearly dropped the turkey. Gabby was sat there in shock. She had no idea that was coming; she was also well aware of the fact that everyone was staring at her waiting for her response. She said, yes. Then everyone was hugging and in tears. Carl then phoned Gabby's parents to ask Walter for his permission. Walter said he was fine with it and then Gabby spoke to both her parents and also Florence who was at the house for Christmas.

It was a different kind of day. There was lots of hugging and kissing and tears. Freda was already talking about buying a new hat. It didn't feel real at all. It was a total surprise to Gabby. She hadn't even realised that Carl had been taking rings out of her jewellery box to try to work out the right size.

CHAPTER 45

The wedding planning came next. It was a bit of
a whirlwind. They set the date for the following
September and sorted themselves out a budget.
Carl likes his spreadsheets. Gabby asked
Florence to be her bridesmaid and both her
nephews to be page boys. She had wanted to be
married at her local church in England but Carl's
family was a lot bigger so they planned to have
it on the Island. Gabby set out looking at
wedding magazines, getting ideas and working
out what they could do for their own wedding.
Gabby wanted her mum involved with choosing
the dress. She arranged to go dress hunting with
her. The dress came from a shop that was owned
by some friends of theirs who lived next door to
where Gabby and Florence had lived before the
accident. The girls had also taught the lady's
children to ride. They remained close friends so
Gabby knew she wanted to get her dress from
her shop.She knew what she wanted in her mind
and going in that shop, she literally tried on two
or three dresses and found the one she wanted.
It was a skirt, narrow and straight, and a fitted
strapless bodice with a short-length, long-
sleeved jacket.

She also chose a veil and a train that would flow behind her chair. She chose the colour for the bridesmaid dress as Aubergine, a dark maroon colour. Florence came shopping with them to look at bridesmaid dresses. Gabby wanted her to choose something she wanted and something she could also wear again.

Gabby got the dress, and a wrap, with shoes that were being dyed the colour of the dress and it was all coming together.

To keep the cost down they both made the invites and all the order of services. They printed them off in their spare room and spent ages putting them together with the ribbon they had. The invites went out and the day of the wedding came.

It was a wet day and Gabby and Walter were picked up from the apartment by a carriage and two grey ponies. They drove the short distance to the town church.

Gabby was really nervous and insisted on talking about anything but what they were doing. Walter just started talking about the prices of hay. Gabby was feeling sick. She was panicking; she was scared of the thought of everyone staring at her in the church and worried about speaking in front of them all. What if she said the wrong words?

She went down the aisle and Carl was waiting for her.

Walter did the handing her over aspect and then stepped back. She sat there whilst the vicar did his first part of the wedding. He then looked at Gabby and looked like he was trying to say something but making funny facial expressions and hand movements.

She couldn't think what he was on about when he came out with, 'Your veil, you need to lift it.' Oops. She had totally forgotten that bit. She was feeling quite good hidden away under her piece of material.

The wedding went by in a blur. Gabby was stunned. She had done it. She didn't see much of her new husband that night; he was busy with his friends. Gabby spent her time with her sister. They chatted about the day and they talked about the people there who neither of them knew and laughed at the way people were dancing.

That night, Gabby and Carl left to go on their honeymoon in Russia. It was a place where Gabby had always wanted to visit. It was a long journey and they arrived in the night, so they didn't get to see anything on the way to the hotel. They just got ready for bed and woke to find themselves in the most beautiful place, surrounded in deep snow everywhere.

Being in Russia gave her some strange feelings. They spent half of the trip in Moscow and then they took an overnight train to St Petersburg.

They visited the Winter Palace which had been
a home of the royal family. As Gabby went
around the palace, she had a deep sense of being
there before. This place wasn't new to her. She
saw things in the palace she recognised. She'd
never experienced this before and she was
wondering if this was due to a past life. The
whole country was beautiful and Gabby would
have been very happy staying there. It felt like
home.

They travelled home to the Island after two
weeks and Gabby started a new job. She was
working in a bank again but this time the team
were lovely and she was happier being there.

CHAPTER 46

Three months after they were married, Gabby started feeling unwell; she had a lot of upset stomachs. And the doctors were saying it was a tummy bug but it was persistent. She went back to the doctors and saw a different GP who asked for a urine sample. Gabby did this and the doctor checked it.
He said, 'You don't have a tummy bug, Gabby.'
She said, 'What's wrong with me?'
He said, 'You're pregnant.'
She couldn't believe it. She was on the pill and they had used protection. So, she had no idea she could be pregnant. She was scared and told the doctor he could tell Carl. The doctor went to fetch Carl from the waiting room and told him. It didn't go down very well. They left the doctors with an appointment for the following day. They drove home in silence. It was totally different from what you see on television when the father is over the moon with the news. Gabby had always wanted children but Carl hadn't so it was an awkward situation. Gabby told Carl she would be keeping the baby.

For Gabby, it felt like a miracle, she had always wanted to have children but never knew if it would happen due to her injury. Carl had said he had never really thought about having them so she was worried. She knew that it wasn't going to be easy but she was ready to do what she could to make sure this little life inside her had the best chance possible to be fit and healthy.

Although Florence had her boys, Gabby had absolutely no idea how things happened and it was all a bit daunting. She also had to help the hospital on the Island as they had never had anyone with a spinal injury have a baby before. She had direct contact with her spinal unit in England. They worked with her and the hospital on the Island to keep them fully informed of everything they needed to know.

Being pregnant was a challenge with a spinal injury. Gabby had to go with Carl to the doctors to discuss what happened next. She asked what she should do with regards to all the medication she was taking. The doctor said she could stay on it but that would mean the baby would be born addicted to them, so they would have to wean baby off them when born. Gabby was horrified at that thought and told her doctor she would stop taking all her medication.

She went completely cold turkey. It was a difficult time. The lack of medication made life hard and getting through each day was awful but she wanted to keep the baby safe.

As the baby grew, the ability to get to sleep at night wasn't good. She'd have to turn herself using her arms as normal but now she had the added weight of a little person growing inside her, and moving around was awkward and uncomfortable. All her moving about was keeping Carl awake so Gabby spent a lot of time during her pregnancy sleeping on the sofa so he could have a good night's sleep. This was a regular occurrence during pregnancy.

During the pregnancy, Gabby was worried that something would go wrong when she was alone but that didn't happen. She went in one day to find out that her blood pressure wasn't good and they were told they wanted to start her off. At that moment, she was in shock, thinking, they will soon have a baby and she wasn't ready. What if she couldn't do it?

Before they were taken into the room, Gabby gave the birthing plan to the doctors. She had written on it that if anything happens, to put her to sleep and get the baby out. In no circumstances did she want an epidural because of having an injection in her back. Being paralysed already, she didn't want to lose any more sensation.

They got to the birthing room and Gabby transferred onto the short bed. She was induced and the midwife told her this would make the pain stronger. Gabby was determined to go through it with no pain relief. She concentrated on her breathing to try to get through the pain. Carl was walking around the room picking things up and trying to work out what they were for and eating peanut M&Ms. He was talking and munching and the smell was making Gabby feel sick. She had to tell him to stop as he was making her feel ill.

She had been going through the breathing exercises for about five and a half hours and the nurses came in and out of the room to check the vital signs of the baby on the monitor. The nurse came to check on things and suddenly slammed her hand on the emergency button and started ripping the cords out of the wall.

Within seconds, loads of people came into the room. Gabby was taken straight to the theatre. The umbilical cord had got wrapped around the baby's neck and they needed to get it out straight away. Carl had to wait outside. Gabby was put to sleep and they got the baby out. As soon as the baby was checked over and all was well, they passed the new baby to Carl who was now a father of a son.

He then got left alone with this new little person whilst the doctors and nurses took care of Gabby.

She was bleeding a lot and they had to sort it out before taking her to the recovery room.

Waking up in the recovery room, Gabby saw Carl standing there saying, 'We've got a baby boy.'

He handed her the small baby. They had discussed names and their new addition was called Lloyd. He was perfect.

Gabby spent a week in the hospital due to the caesarean and she found it helpful to have the nurses around as the breastfeeding was hard. She felt useless at it. Something that was supposedly natural and the best thing possible was incredibly difficult. Because Gabby had lost so much blood during the caesarean, this was affecting the milk. She felt like a failure. She stuck with it for five and a half weeks and then had to top up with baby milk from a bottle to make sure Lloyd got all the goodness he needed. During this time she also had to have a few blood transfusions because she'd lost so much blood and was lacking. She was very pale and felt weak. She wasn't keen on having the transfusions because she was scared of catching something but was told she was totally safe. She didn't have a choice, she had to make sure she got strong again so she could care for their new baby. Lloyd was very popular in the hospital, the nurses loved him.

Gabby would wake up in the night hearing babies crying, expecting to need to feed him and he would be out of the room. The nurse said she took him out to help her get some sleep. They had been having cuddles in the nurse's room. In the hospital she had the best midwife. She was so well looked after and Lloyd was much loved. They were given plenty of time to get things ready for getting home and Gabby was taught how to bathe Lloyd, how to hold him and lots of other tips. She never felt rushed out of the hospital and the time recovering from the caesarean gave both Gabby and Carl time to learn things they hadn't done before.

CHAPTER 47

When she and Lloyd were allowed home, they were scared. Being away from the hospital and now fully responsible for this little person. This feeling changed at home; they got into a routine, and Gabby did everything she possibly could to care, cuddle and love this little person. She felt like the luckiest person in the world. After all the bad stuff that had gone on, this little person was a true gift from above. She couldn't explain the love she felt for him.

She put him in a carrier strapped to her to move around the house to keep him safe. She soon learnt to do things her way, motherly care the sitting-down way. Lloyd slept in Gabby and Carl's bedroom in his cot. It was good for when he woke for feeds. She'd get him changed, fed and put him back into his bed. She'd sometimes sit and watch him sleep. This little perfect boy was part of her and he was amazing.

As Lloyd grew, he went into his own room. Even at such a young age, he pulled himself up, which helped Gabby get him out of the cot. He wasn't walking or talking but she was sure he knew things were different for her and he was helping her.

Gabby couldn't reach properly to use the bath so to bathe Lloyd she set up a washing up bowl on the top of the ironing board, she generally got very wet too.

Yvette travelled to the Island after a couple of weeks. She hadn't been able to see him before due to having a skin condition that could have been passed on to Lloyd via the healing umbilical cord. As soon as this came off, the doctor said it was safe.

It was amazing for Yvette to be there and finally meet her third grandson. She was a big help and she'd look after Lloyd, allowing Gabby time to have a bath or a lie-down. They would take him for walks in his pram with Grandma Yvette pushing the pram proudly. This was something that Gabby was gutted about not being able to do. Not being able to walk around pushing her new baby. She had to keep reminding herself that she had to do it her way and her way to Lloyd was completely normal. He knew nothing about what able-bodied mums do as he didn't have one.

During the crawling stage, Gabby had wondered what she would do if he went somewhere that she couldn't get to. But despite the fact that if he had wanted to, he could have done exactly that, he never did. Even when he started walking, he never ran away from her. He always listened. He was the most loving little boy.

She would do lots of reading, colouring and playing with him. It was a special time and she wanted to make the most of every minute. After five months, Gabby had to go back to work. They had spent ages trying to find a suitable childminder. They found a lady who lived in the same village as them and who was married to someone Carl played in a band with. She and her family were to be Lloyd's second family. She was brilliant with him. She wrote daily diaries of everything they did. She took him to toddler groups and the zoo. She took photos of the days they spent together. Gabby went to work in tears; leaving Lloyd was really painful. She wanted to be with him and leaving him for the day was ripping her heart out. It was horrible. She knew she had no choice. They had a mortgage to pay and they wanted to make sure that they could do nice things with Lloyd.

CHAPTER 48

A few years later, they had saved up the money to go to America. The previous Christmas Gabby bought Carl a voucher for him to do the world's highest skydive, 18,000ft, which was in Florida. It was a really hot day and Lloyd and Gabby just hung out whilst Carl had the lessons before going in the plane to do the jump. They sat waiting with the camera poised to take pictures as soon as Carl came in sight.

When they were waiting, a very good-looking man came over to her and asked if she wanted to have a go. It must have been the mesmerizing looks of this Italian man that did it because before she knew it, she had agreed to do the jump. This was a big deal. Gabby was terrified of heights and also terrified of flying.

By the time Carl landed, Gabby was dressed in a jumpsuit ready to do the next jump. Carl was shocked. The talk with the instructor and the team went that on landing they would run to help lift Gabby's legs and set them down gently. They got in the plane and Gabby's instructor checked everything she was wearing and was talking to her the whole time.

They were right next to the door which was scary. When it was their turn they sat on the edge of the plane and then toppled out. A wave of panic hit her as she was out. A feeling of being out of control. She had to tell herself, 'Don't panic, don't panic.'

They had 90 seconds of freefall and her instructor was very good. He talked to her the whole time and she managed to let go of the straps and put her arms out and look around at the views. When the parachute went out and they shot up in the air, one of Gabby's legs flew up in the air. Then they were peacefully floating down. They chatted to each other and the instructor pointed out all the different places of interest.

Coming in to land was faster than she was expecting. They could see the people ready to catch them but they came down so fast they didn't get to them in time. On landing, Gabby's left leg got caught underneath and it felt horrible.

Having a different sensation, she just felt odd. Then wow, she'd just done the world's highest skydive and it was amazing. She was thrilled that she had done it. That afternoon, they went to a nice place for lunch and during that, Gabby was feeling really odd.

She started feeling sick and she mentioned it to Carl, who said, 'What on Earth would it cost if we went to the hospital in America?'
So, they went to a large shop and got some leg supports and painkillers, believing she'd just wrenched herself.

A couple of days after, Gabby's leg went black. She said to Carl that she really needed to get it checked. Carl told her she'd better find out where to go. So, she checked out the welcome pack at the house they were staying in and found the details for the hospital.
They went along and it was a very different experience. It was like being in an office rather than a hospital. Gabby had an x-ray and the doctor told her she had broken her femur. He said it needed operating on but as they were on holiday he would put a splint on it and they had to go straight to the hospital when they got back to the Island.
This had happened on the second day of a sixteen-day holiday. It was a difficult time, trying to hide the fact that she was in so much pain every single day. She didn't want to ruin the holiday for Carl. So, she tried to ignore it. They continued with the holiday. Carl went on all the rides and Gabby took Lloyd to see characters whilst they waited, and then he went on some of the children's rides.

When it was time to go home, they had to drop off their bags with the airline and when Carl told them about Gabby's leg, things took some time for them to agree to let her travel. It was a long and painful journey. When they got back to the Island, Carl thought it would be best to wait till after the bank holiday to go to the hospital because of the queues.

So, on Tuesday, he went off to work and Gabby went to the hospital with Freda, Les and Lloyd. They took all the details and she gave them the paperwork and x-rays from the hospital in America. She was admitted to the hospital for an operation on her femur. The operation went well. Her leg was fixed and it had to be left out straight for a long time.

After six weeks, she had the plaster removed and was allowed to bend it. But by then, the leg had healed straight and wasn't happy about bending. This was hard and took weeks and weeks of physio sessions and her mother-in-law massaging it for her.

Gabby was told that because of the break she was no longer able to play basketball. Because if the ball hit her leg it could break it. This was a huge blow. This was the one and only activity she did for herself. And she was in a team with her work.

During the recovery time, she was working from home.

It wasn't ideal but it was better than not having something to keep her going. When her leg was healed, she finally went back to work and carried on with everyday life.

CHAPTER 49

To Gabby, working in an office was like being a caged animal. She felt the need to be outside whatever the weather and not stuck in a room going cross-eyed looking at a computer screen all day. This wasn't what her life should be like. Reality dictated that she didn't have a huge amount of options with regards to working from a wheelchair. Her wonderful outdoor life had come to an abrupt end. Even now, it felt to her that she was grieving for that life, her friends and the horse and farming world.

Because of the ups and downs of her life and the feeling of depression, she felt she wanted to have Hypnotherapy. This was to help her to cope with the years of turmoil and hate she carried about her accident. She knew that it was hurting her and she wanted to do something about it. Hanging on to so much hate and bad thoughts were only hurting her and she was going through her day feeling robbed of the life she had. The more she thought that, the worse she felt. When you go through these feelings, it's not the person you are focusing on that is hurt.

They literally have no idea what you are going through; you are ultimately just hurting yourself.

This was what Gabby was doing for years and she needed to break this very destructive cycle. She went to weekly sessions that were incredibly emotional and draining but they went through so much. She was taken back to the accident and was able to let go of the negative feelings she had about it all.

She was able to contact the lady she had been working for and for whom she had hated for years and asked to meet her. She agreed to meet and discussed the accident and the hypnotherapy and how things were from her point of view. There were a lot of misunderstandings and a lot of tears. But there were hugs and friendships remade. This was a good thing for Gabby's mind and wellbeing.

CHAPTER 50

When Gabby had all that time at home, she
became totally obsessed with skydiving. All she
could do was look at skydiving photos and read
all she could online about it and the thought that
she had done this was still crazy in her mind.
One website she came across was a lady making
skydiving jewellery. Her name was Christine
and she made necklaces using skydiving closure
pins. Gabby thought this would be a good
Christmas present for Carl, so she got in touch
with Christine and they chatted about the
present and as they got chatting about what had
happened, they struck up a friendship. Gabby
asked Christine to make Carl and herself a
necklace each in the colours of the canopy they
had on that day. They came in plenty of time for
Christmas and they were amazing. From that
chance meeting online, over many, many miles,
a new friendship was born.
Christine was a wonderful lady. She and Gabby
spoke via email a huge amount.

Gabby would write and tell her about everything that was happening with her and she would tell Gabby about all the things she and her husband do within the skydiving world and it all sounded amazing. They kept in touch.

On their next holiday, they decided to make it to Florida again, this time near to where Christine and her husband David lived. They arranged to meet up and spend some time together. Lloyd totally fell in love with Christine and remains a huge fan of their wonderful friend. Lloyd has a picture of himself with them in a frame next to the side of his bed.

Christine and David were once-in-a-lifetime friends, who were truly the most welcoming, kind people you could ever choose to meet. They invited them into their home and they had many amazing times together. This amazing friendship came after a freak accident leading to a broken leg. It makes you think. Everything happens for a reason, even if we don't see it at the time.

Gabby told Christine how she would like to do another skydive, but to do it where she didn't break any bones. Christine put her in touch with Cris who she'd been chatting to for a long time about how she could do a tandem skydive with minimal risk of injury. She wanted to do at least one skydive where she was in one piece at the end of it. The only thing that was stopping her was Carl.

He was not happy about it at all. He kept going on about the time off work she had and how difficult it was for the family when she wasn't fully mobile. But this was something that Gabby felt she needed to do. To prove to herself that she could do it.

Carl finally agreed, so at the end of that year's holiday, they went to the drop zone to do Gabby's tandem skydive with Cris, Christine and David. All of them would jump together and they made it a time to remember. The jump went well. Gabby was very nervous after the outcome of the other jump but she knew she would never be satisfied until she'd gone through with it. Cris looked after her and they landed with no problems or broken bones.

Lloyd started nursery that year and he was attending the nursery attached to the school he would later attend. He was ready for this, he was at the stage where he needed to be mixing with children his own age and he ws learning things fast.

He quickly made friends, got on well with the routine and would go to the childminders after he finished and Gabby and Carl would pick him up on their way home. At the childminders she also had other children she looked after so Lloyd had friends to play with after school too.

As well as those children, the child minder had her own family. Two girls and a boy. They were also brilliant with the children their mum was taking care of. To Lloyd it was like he had two sisters and a brother in this second family. He spent more time with them than he did with Gabby and Carl. It was hard having to leave him each day but being in this family home after school they knew he was safe and happy. And his happiness was the most important thing, then came the mortgage and living expenses.

CHAPTER 51

Back on the Island, work and school life continued. Lloyd carried on doing well at school and work carried on just being the daily grind. Gabby decided to move to a different department within her work. She went to the interview with crystals tucked into her bra for good luck. They were supposed to touch the skin and she was worried about pressure sores if she'd put them somewhere she couldn't feel. She was given the job. The work was interesting, the people were really nice and she loved it. She felt happy at work again after so long. Going to work being happy made such a big difference. It may have only been a different department but it felt like a totally different bank. She'd been at this job for just a couple of weeks when she went out one lunchtime and came back to work. Pushing into the reception area, there were patterned cobbles on the ground and they were quite lumpy to wheel across. When Gabby was pushing into the building, one of her wheels got caught in a gap and she shot out of her chair onto the ground. She hit the ground really hard. She lay there and was rapidly surrounded by people asking if everything was okay.

The pain was horrific. She knew something was wrong.

Someone called an ambulance and she was given a coat as a pillow and one over her as the shock was making her feel cold and sick. The ambulance came and Gabby's new boss came to the hospital with her.

She was really worried about losing her job because of this. Gabby's boss was lovely, saying, 'Absolutely not at all.'

A colleague phoned Carl and told him that Gabby had an accident and to meet her at the hospital. After being checked over by the doctors and having x-rays, she was told she'd broken her hip and she needed an operation. She couldn't believe it. She couldn't stop apologising to her boss for the fact that she'd be off work and she'd only just started this position. She had the operation to put some kind of metalwork in to keep her hip in the right place. And so, more time off work.

This injury put a stop to any more ideas of skydiving for Gabby.

When she went back to work after a few months, she had lost her nerve pushing around and transfers were difficult and painful. She was given a parking space under her work building and had to call for someone to come out to the car and be their when she got out for her safety. She also didn't venture outside at all after that.

She was scared of injuring herself again. She never really got her confidence back for going out into town and shopping like she had done before. Online shopping became her best friend.

CHAPTER 52

On a morning in January she was at work busily working away, she had a phone call from Walter. It was very strange because her dad never rang her. If they needed anything, Yvette would always be the one to call. So, it was very odd. Walter said that he'd been to the hospital and they had told him he has pancreatic cancer and that Gabby was not to worry, as they can treat it and he'll be okay.

On hearing this news, Gabby was in floods of tears, begging him to get on with her mum as he wasn't always the easiest person to live with and was not very nice to Yvette a lot of the time. It took a lot of calming down to continue with her work that day. Over the next couple of days, Walter got progressively worse. He was taken into the hospital as he was not well at all. Gabby had said to her mum to call any time, day or night. For Gabby, being so far away felt awful. She wanted to be with her mum and dad at this time but she had Carl and Lloyd to think about and couldn't just leave them. Carl had said he was sure it'll be fine and it was probably more drama than it actually was. So, she carried on and Yvette kept her informed.

During that next night, they had a phone call from the hospital saying Gabby needed to get there straight away, she was told she had been put down as the next of kin. She told the nurse that she lived on the Island and that she would call her mum. For Gabby this was terrifying and she felt like it wasn't really happening, like it was some really bad dream.

Not to her dad, the dad that took them to school, riding lessons, pony club rallies, and gave them everything. He was there when she had her accident and despite all the years of struggles, he was always there in the background.

She phoned her mum and told her she needed to get to the hospital but she couldn't get there that night and thankfully they managed to sort Walter out and get him settled. Due to the cancer he had, he turned yellow. The treatment in the hospital dealt with this and they sent him home. We all saw this as something positive. On talking to Yvette, she told Gabby that Walter would get angry a lot of the time. Shouting at her for not cutting up the bread for his egg and soldiers in the right way. It was hurtful stuff and Walter was never one to apologise.

A few days at home and Walter told Yvette to get him a drink. He was rude and on making the drink he told her that she would have to give it to him because he couldn't do it.

She didn't realise the enormity of that until later on. She was just trying to get through the emotion of it all. Then he went to the toilet and shouted at her that he needed help.

He said, 'I can't wipe, this stupid hand won't work and I can't walk.'

Yvette went to help him and got her walker and dragged him back on it to the bed. She then phoned the ambulance. Walter had had a stroke. When he was at the hospital, he was very ill. He had a massive heart attack and that's when Gabby got a phone call from Florence saying she needed to come home. She rang her mum in the hospital and said she'll be back as soon as possible. Yvette handed her phone to Walter so Gabby could speak to her dad. She told him she loved him and would be back as soon as she could get there.

She tried everything she could to get off the Island but it was a nightmare. There were no hire cars with hand controls so she couldn't fly, so she had to book an overnight ferry and take her car. The morning of her leaving, she had a phone call from her mum, Walter had passed away. She hadn't got home in time.

She felt like her whole world had fallen apart. Life suddenly felt very scary. She didn't know how she was going to carry on without him. She was in bits. Sat on the side of the bed. Carl came around the side and said she wasn't to cry in front of Lloyd and upset him.

When your dad dies, this isn't an easy thing to do. She had to suck it up and tell Lloyd that his Grandpa had passed away.

He said to Gabby, 'Mummy, aren't you sad Grandpa has died?'

She told him she was very sad and that Daddy had wanted her to be strong and not to upset him. He was such a star as always. That night, she was on the overnight ferry to England to go and help her mum.

She stayed there for three weeks, sorting out all the paperwork with her and organising the funeral and everything that goes along with it when someone passes away. Walter and Yvette didn't have any money, so Yvette was in a panic about the funeral. Gabby said she'd pay for it all. She wanted to take away as much worry from her as she physically could. The funeral was hard-going. Gabby did the eulogy and at the time of writing it, she didn't really think about how hard it would be to speak in front of all the people in church on the day. She did it though, as hard as it was. She was very glad she did it. When they were in the church, there was a butterfly flying around and it kept flying by Yvette, Florence and Gabby. It was unusual as it was February and it was very cold, damp and windy. They all believe that it was Walter, showing them he was still with them.

They had a lot of friends come to the funeral but Gabby couldn't remember who was there at all. Lisa had come and she stayed with Gabby for the whole of the wake. There was a full village hall of people but she couldn't tell you who was actually there.

The bottom fell out of her world the day Walter died and she was struggling to figure out how things could ever be the same again.

CHAPTER 53

Life continued and work was good. They had a
new building that was being built and the whole
bank was going to change. One drawback was
that Gabby wasn't going to have a parking
space, which was something that worried her.
She mentioned it to her HR department and they
said, 'What makes you think you're more
deserving of a parking space than anyone else?'
So, after speaking to them at length, it was
agreed she'd start work at 7 am so she could find
a space every morning nearby.

Work changed in the new building, the team had
changed and the line managers changed. From
the point of view of those doing the admin, it
wasn't a good change; it was like going
backwards, not making progress. It literally
ruined the job. They couldn't get to know clients
along with their managers because they were
doing the admin for every manager on the floor
and as each day went by, they never knew who
they were going to be helping. But she had to
remind herself it paid the bills. She stuck at it
along with her colleagues.

Everyone knows change can be hard.

At work, you get told to embrace the change and this was okay, but the change really wasn't on the work side as it was more of the management side that affected a lot of them. Suddenly, there were lots of people off with stress and so many people leaving. Also, a time of huge redundancy, which was frightening for everyone and totally out of the blue. Lots of whispering during that time and people crying. It was a horrible time for everyone but especially those who found they no longer had a job to go to. Gabby found that she was not enjoying her work anymore; the whole place had got so big. They didn't feel like a team anymore. She found she was getting stressed and went to the doctor who signed her off to get back on track. She spent a lot of time thinking about things and being away from the cause of the stress was good but when she got nearer to the time of going back, she was getting panicky again.

A day or two before going back to work she'd sorted things out, spoken to some of her colleagues and was ready to go back.

Her thoughts were always on how to get through the days. How to ignore what people were saying to her. Reading self-help books on how to cope with bullying and becoming more positive. All of this was creating negative thoughts, and the more negative the thoughts, the more negativity came back to her from the universe.

That night, she was getting ready for bed. She had transferred onto the bed and Lloyd had woke up with a bad dream; so she went into his room and talked to him and read some of his bedtime storybooks to him.

She left him settled and went back to the bedroom to get back on the bed. Carl was in the lounge still at this point. She transferred as she normally would next to the bed. But she lost her balance and fell from the bed onto the floor.

As she went down, her right leg got caught up underneath her and made an awful crunching sound. She screamed and Carl and Lloyd both rushed into the bedroom. Gabby couldn't move and was in terrible pain. Carl had to move her chair to get to her and picked her up back onto the bed. She mentioned there had been an awful sound as she hit the floor but Carl said perhaps she'd landed on a coat hanger.

She knew in her mind, and the fact that there wasn't a coat hanger on the floor, that this wasn't it. Carl and Lloyd stayed with her and told her to rest and calm down. Gabby and Carl's bed was pretty high and sitting on the edge of it, her feet weren't able to touch the floor. They checked Gabby's skin. Nothing was grazed, which was good. And checked for any obvious bruising and couldn't see anything.

So, Carl thought they should give it a day or two and see how it was then and if no better by the weekend then they'd get it checked.

The next couple of days were awful, she was so uncomfortable and in so much pain. By Saturday, she said to Carl that she really thought she needed to get her leg checked. So, she went to A & E. When they were checked in, they asked when she had hurt herself and she said it was the Thursday and they wanted to know why they had left it until the Saturday before coming. They said they had hoped it was just bruised.

She then went to have an x-ray which was excruciating. After that, she was taken to wait in a little room in A & E to see what the doctor saw on the x-rays. The doctor checked the x-rays and came in to inform Gabby she had broken her right femur this time. She had to have an operation to fix it.

So, another stay in the hospital. This made her feel very down. She couldn't believe that yet another incident had come along and messed with everything. The doctors were amazing and they did things so much more different than when she had broken the left femur. They didn't put a plaster on, so after the operation, she was able to get back into her normal chair and get about.

She felt very weak and it was massively painful but the doctor said it was safe and it'll just take time to recover.

She was really the world's worst patient. After being in the spinal unit, she turned into a monster as soon as she had the hospital wristband on. She questioned everything and always checked everything they gave her and questioned why they were doing things to her. She wasn't sure if the doctors were annoyed with her for always questioning them or happy that someone was not going to just sit there and not question something if they believe it to be wrong or to ask them why they are doing something in a way she wasn't used to.

This injury was well-managed. After the operation, she had no intention of staying in the hospital another night. She pretty much insisted they should use the bed for truly ill people and it would be in their best interests to send her home and she promised that if there were any issues, she'd go back. They agreed. She did feel terrible but she didn't want another night in the hospital. Being at home, she could rest easier and recover in comfort. She went back for her check-ups and all was fine. She just needed recovery time. During the recovery process, Gabby tried to get her mind back on being calm about work stuff.

This was all she had in life. Her life out of work revolved around Lloyd and Carl's hobbies. She didn't have that for herself.

With losing Walter and all the stresses around her she began looking into what else was out there. She had many years before been introduced to angels, through a friend but hadn't done anything more. She believed they existed but didn't do anything about discovering more. She decided she wanted to change that, to see what would happen for her if she worked with the universe and the angels in her life. She was on a spiritual path now and it was making her feel connected and calm with it and helped her focus on what she wanted to do workwise so perhaps this could be the next chapter. The life she wanted for herself was perhaps not where she was now. She had started doing mindfulness meditation.

When things got less painful, she went back to work again. Keeping everything crossed to keep her body intact after so many incidents along the way.

CHAPTER 54

Being back in the office was making her unwell. She was trying to get through each day just by doing it rather than living. It was something that needed to change. She needed to make a change or her life would be on a spiral of being negative and attracting more negativity. This lead to her handing her notice in on a job she'd been in for twelve years. It was a scary prospect but something she was doing for herself to find the path she needed to be on.

After all the trials and tribulations along the way, Gabby had been sent a book from a friend, which talked about the Law of Attraction. How what you feel brings more of that feeling to you and that you have to be careful about what you wish for as that may well manifest into something you accidentally asked for, unconsciously manifesting it. She began to learn about this more and was told about how we all have guardian angels. She'd read about people who had connections with their angels and even those who could see them.

She wanted to learn more about it so she signed up to join a group called the Angel Summer School. She would have to sign in each week at the same time. They could all see each other but they'd all be in different places in the world. Gabby was really nervous to begin with and didn't know if she would be making a fool of herself doing it. All the ladies in the group seemed to have a lot better knowledge than her but she was willing to give it a try. She wrote lots of notes and enjoyed the meditations they did together. They had homework and they were taught how to read Angel cards.

During this time, Gabby started also having 1:1 sessions with The Angel Lady, as she was known in their house. She would call up on a Tuesday every week and talk to Gabby about her life and how things were going. If she thought Gabby needed to focus on certain areas, she would tell her. She also gave her more information on how to make things better for herself.

Working with the Angel Lady, Gabby realised that all that time, she was trying to figure out a path for herself and find out what she was going to do for money. During these sessions, it came to her that proofreading would be the thing she'd start doing. When she focused on this subject and made the intention of manifesting this, things very quickly began to happen.

She had contacted a lady about a book she read that was good but full of mistakes so Gabby offered to send her the errors.

She was a bit concerned to begin with as to how she would take her criticising her work but they took it exactly how she hoped. They asked her to go through it and she sent them the errors. Gabby managed to re-read the book and send the errors within two days.

A day or so later, the daughter of the author who also happened to be an author emailed her and said she has a new book coming out and would she please read through it before it goes to the publishers. She'd had it proofread professionally but wanted a second check.

Gabby was happy to be asked. She read the book in about the same amount of time. She found numerous errors and typed them all up for the lady at the end. The author was incredibly grateful for her help. She was mortified that the errors that were there hadn't been picked up by the professional she had paid.

This was paving the way forward for Gabby. She set the intention that this was the path she was now going to be on. This would allow her to work from home, so she knew she'd always be there for Lloyd and she would be doing something she absolutely loved for a living.

The next day, she had a message from The Angel Lady saying she had been contacted by a friend asking if she knew of a proofreader and was it okay to put them in touch. Gabby felt like she would burst with excitement. She replied straight away saying absolutely, yes, please. She then heard from the publishers who were needing an in-house proofreader and they spoke to Gabby. Gabby told the lady she was doing a course online but she'd just started doing proofreading for authors already and they discussed prices. She was then taken on as the publisher's in-house proofreader. Gabby knew this was down to the angels and manifesting. Learning new ways of thinking and feeling. Meditating and helping others was totally transforming her life.

CHAPTER 55

Gabby then set up her own page on Facebook as this was a great place to advertise and get people to review the work she had already done for them. She spent ages trying to figure out what to call her proofreading business. She decided to meditate and ask her angels for the answer. So, that evening she went in her bedroom after putting Lloyd to bed and put on a meditation and whilst in meditation she asked the angels to help her come up with a name for her company. The following day, the name 'Between the Lines' came to her. She knew straight away that was the sign after asking for advice. She designed a logo for herself and set things up.

Gabby went on to tell her mum how amazing all the angel work was and how the change it can make is so positive and she wanted to share that with her and show her that she can experience those things too. She made friends with the other ladies doing the same sessions. One lady, in particular, was in close contact with her. They felt so connected to each other.

There was a bond there and Gabby and she could see they would always have this closeness and maybe one day, they would be able to work together as they both had the same passion for books. This was something they could both see themselves doing together.

As Gabby went about her day to day life, she now included working on journaling. She wrote a journal about what had happened that day to get all of it out of her system. She also wrote a future diary about how she wanted to manifest her life for the future, and wrote it as if it was actually already like that. She did monthly affirmations and listened to them twice a day, and meditated every evening. Most importantly though, she was in constant communication with her angels.

As the days went by, Gabby gradually got herself into a routine of working on her proofreading side of life and doing her normal household chores. She found that weeks would go by and she wouldn't see anyone except for Carl and Lloyd.
She always kept in touch with her friends she'd been in college with and looked back on that time with so much happiness. She was so happy at that time.

They had such a great life and learnt so much. Her friends felt like family from that time in her life. They were all very close.

When she went back to England she'd make sure she would meet up with as many of them as possible so they could have a catch-up. It was something she held on to. It was really nice as they too had children, so they got to play together or just meet depending on ages. But a new generation getting together, introduced by their parents' friendship. How life had turned out for them all was so different from how they all thought but no matter what life threw at them, they were always still there for each other.

CHAPTER 56

During her life so far, she had so many accidents and terrible incidents. The horrific spinal injury, broken bones, and the violent boyfriend. These things were all manifested in some way, albeit unconsciously.

Gabby had a long way to go on her journey but this was the end of one journey and the start of another.

Gabby had contacted the hospital after all her injuries and asked if it was okay if she went to use the physio and get things going again for herself. They were more than happy for her to do this. She continued with her intention setting each month and set the intention that she will be walking again. This seemed like a big ask but as you ask for something, you don't have to know how it can happen and you just need to believe it will. So, this is what Gabby went on to do. She would have to spend a certain amount of time in England and then she'd go back to the Island for the rest of the week.

This worked out fine as Carl was working from home and Lloyd was busy with school and they both understood how much this meant to Gabby.

Gabby wanted to work on keeping her body in shape for when the time came where she'd be able to walk again.

When she was in the hospital, she tried walking with callipers. They put them on her and put her between parallel bars. She was told to swing her body through and use her arms to lift herself. She wasn't happy about this. She wanted to be doing a walking motion, not swinging. Who swings in normal life? She spent a lot of time in between the bars doing as much of it as she could. The callipers were awkward to put on and when she had them on, she felt like she was going to tip forward and her legs being kept straight would just mean that she would end up flat on her face. Every day, she tried and it became easier. The physio department was always busy but as most of the people in there couldn't walk, Gabby could go in to practice whenever she wanted to.

During the day, Gabby would work on proofreading for people and she loved that work so much. Books were her passion and she thoroughly enjoyed this new direction she had taken.

This was something she took with her to the hospital and some days she'd plug her laptop in in the cafe and work on her business, then go and do more physio work.

This was working really well. She also volunteered to help newly-injured patients. This was something she could really work hard on. And could totally understand the different reactions from people, especially after her own very angry reaction to what had happened to her.

She was going in each day to the hospital for at least two hours a day. She'd spend that in the physio, going through the bars, then be back in her chair. She was working on the fact that all the positive thoughts she could keep coming in her mind and all the positive results of the work on the callipers would manifest more positivity her way. She held on to this belief with both hands.

One day, she was sitting in the cafe catching up with some work and a young girl came in. She had bought a drink and was looking around for a space to sit. Gabby moved her things over and asked if she wanted to join her. The girl was shy but said thank you and came slowly over. The young girl looked very pale, she had a back brace on and she had a very sad look on her face. Gabby gave her a warm smile and introduced herself. She asked the girl her name, it was Rose.

She told Gabby she had a car accident. That she was driving along and it was dark, a person coming towards her was driving with their headlights on full beam and she couldn't see. For that brief moment of blindness, she turned the car and her wheels clipped the curb. She had been going about 50 M.P.H.; this flipped her car over and it hit a tree. She was on her own in the car.

The person with the bright headlights didn't stop and she was stuck in the car whilst fire crew had to cut her out. She was finding it all so overwhelming. Gabby sat and listened whilst the young girl poured it all out. This is what people need. No commenting, no comparisons, just someone to sit and listen to how a person is feeling and let them get it all out.

She sat and listened to Rose for what felt like about half an hour. But two hours later, they were both still sat chatting. Gabby interrupted just for a moment and went to get them both a drink. Rose was happy to accept and she continued to tell Gabby what her life had been like before that night. She'd been studying to be a hairdresser but now she didn't know how her dreams were going to work out. Gabby told her to try and focus on things that were happening in the present time.

That she was totally new to this injury and as hard as it is to forget life outside the hospital, she needed to think of her wellbeing and recovery above everything else. From her own experience, she knew this wasn't something that was easy and she knew there would be lots of times when Rose would want to scream, shout and cry but for now, she needed to just concentrate on herself.

They were just finishing their drinks and a nurse came over to say Rose needed to go and have some physio. Gabby told her she'd be in the hospital every week and if she wanted to talk then she'd be happy to. They swapped numbers and then Rose had to leave.

Gabby sat back, watching her go, remembering with such clarity of the time when that was her. And looking at things now, how far she had come. She wanted to support these patients and show them things she'd done and share stories. But mostly, she wanted to be there to listen and give hugs when needed.

CHAPTER 57

When Gabby went back to her room that night, she did a video call with Carl and Lloyd and told them about meeting Rose. She had not thought about anything else since meeting her. She just wished there was more she could do for her. Carl just told her that being there for her was enough and that was bigger than she thought. Lloyd told her he had been doing some cooking at school and had made a pasta dish which he had taken home that night and they'd had it for tea. It turned out really well and he told Gabby he would make it when she got home so she could try it too.

Before going to sleep that night, Gabby switched on her meditation app on her phone and sat listening to a meditation for manifestation. She sat on her bed and relaxed and listened to the guided session. She focused on manifesting her being able to walk again. The meditation went through relaxing her body, focusing on her breathing and removing negative thoughts from her mind.

Taking her to a place where she would see a blackboard where all the negative thoughts and words that she had thought and people have said to her in the past were written. She had to go to the board and take the wiper and remove the negative comments. These would then be dust on the floor, seeped down into the earth and therefore removing the negative thoughts. She then had to write on the board the positive thoughts that would help her manifest her dreams. These thoughts would then be what she would think of instead of the usual negativity. Whilst in this state of meditation, Gabby literally felt her body become lighter and a new optimistic feeling ran through her.

She went to sleep that night feeling happy and knowing things would be fine and she'd get to where she needed to at the right time.

She had one more day at the hospital this week then she'd be off back to the Island. She drove to the hospital and parked up outside the spinal unit. She got her things out of the car and went straight down to the physio to start her calliper session.

When she got into the physio department, there were so many people in there. It was hard to get past all the chairs over to the bars. When she reached the bars, she put her laptop and bags down out the way and went to get the callipers out of the cupboard. She put them on and wheeled into the bars.

Putting her feet on the floor, she pulled herself up and did a few walks up and down the bars. She was making her way back towards her chair when her phone started ringing. She frantically tried to get to it before it rang off. She got to her chair but she had no way of taking the call until she'd sat down. If she let go with one hand, she'd fall. She turned herself around and backed up onto her chair.

As she sat down, her phone stopped ringing. Typical, she thought to herself. She decided she'd take her callipers off, go to the cafe, get a drink, do a bit of work and then make her way back to the harbour to get on the boat to go home.

She ordered herself a hot chocolate and took it over to a table and got her laptop out ready to work for a couple of hours before leaving.

The hot chocolate was steaming hot and she had a tiny sip. The warm liquid was piping hot and she could feel it burning her tongue; it was very sweet and definitely what she needed after her walking session.

She opened her emails to see what had come in for her. She noticed an email from someone she didn't recognise. She clicked on the email and saw it to be a manuscript from an author in America. The lady had written about her family life and wanted Gabby to proofread it for her.

She was super excited; she'd never done any work for someone overseas. This would be a great opportunity and a fantastic experience. She clicked on reply and sent the lady a message to say she'd be happy to take on her work and asked what time frame she needed it to be done by.

Gabby then checked the rest of her emails and spent her time sending replies and finishing her drink. Her inbox had been particularly busy and she saw that the time was ticking on and she needed to get herself ready to go back home. She logged off and put her things back in her bag. She then took her cup back to the counter and thanked them for her drink. She pushed back out of the hospital and out to the car for her long drive to the harbour.

The drive to the harbour took two hours and she switched on the radio to listen to it as she drove. She felt like she had company in the car then, she was in an upbeat mood and sang along to the songs she knew. She got to the harbour as they were opening the check-in. She went straight up and checked in. They told her to drive through and put her hazard lights on when asked to get on the boat to show the crew she needed assistance.

The boat wasn't full that day so they got on quite quickly and everyone settled down into their seats for the four-hour journey.

On the journey, Gabby decided she would just read for pleasure this time. She loved crime books and got totally swept into the story whilst the boat took her back home.

CHAPTER 58

She arrived back and got off the boat, driving towards home to see Carl and Lloyd. They were waiting for her when she arrived and they were all excited to see each other.

They helped Gabby take her bags in and they all went in to get a cuppa and catch up with how things had been going. Lloyd had been doing really well at school and wanted to show Gabby what he'd been doing and telling her about what had been going on with his friends. Carl had been busy with his work and was getting work in faster than his stock was coming in. Things were going well for him.

Gabby told them about the things at the spinal unit and told them a book was hopefully coming her way to proofread for an American lady. Gabby was catching up on her emails whilst drinking a cuppa and chatting. She found a new email had come in from the American lady who was called Isabelle. She had a very exciting life; she had been a dancer in shows and her husband was a scientist. He was researching how to make it possible for people with spinal injuries to walk again.

Gabby couldn't believe what she was reading. This was amazing to hear.

She shouted to Carl, 'Listen to this, the author's husband is working on getting people with spinal cord injuries walking again. What do you think? I think it's fate.'

Carl read the email and he too thought it was interesting. He said not to get too excited about things as this was just a proofreading job. She understood where he was coming from. She just wanted to learn more about it. But she didn't want to feel crushed so she put the thoughts out of her mind and went on to look at the new book Isabelle had sent to her.

The book was long and Gabby really wanted to take her time over it because it was the first book that she'd been looking at that was going to have different spellings and new sayings that aren't used in the United Kingdom, so she'd be needing to check things with Isabelle as she worked through it.

The next day, she had to get Lloyd sorted for his friend Barney to come round. She was taking them bowling and then they were going to have the rest of the afternoon back at the house playing. She picked them up about midday and then drove to the bowling. They ordered lunch there and then would play after.

It wasn't very busy on that day and there were just a couple of lanes occupied. They had their usual hotdog and chips and then went to get signed up to bowl.

Gabby was going to play as well so they all had their names down and took it in turns bowling. Gabby went first and had the sides up to help as she found it tricky throwing the ball being sat down and she needed all the help she could get. She threw the ball, it hit the side of the chair, went diagonally across the lane, pinged on one side and shot to the other side, then trickled to the left, hitting just three pins. The boys watching her found this hilarious. They were all in fits of laughter.

Lloyd went next and threw his ball straight down the middle but it left a split, so he had to try getting them all down in one throw but it was an impossible task, so he aimed for the left side where he knocked them straight down. Barney went next, throwing his off to the right and it knocked down five pins. They all took it in turns and in the end, Lloyd won the first game, followed by Barney then Gabby and Gabby won the second game, followed by Lloyd and then Barney. They all had a lot of fun. They left the bowling and set off back home. Lloyd and Barney were in the car, laughing and chatting all the way home.

When they got home, they all got out of the car. Gabby went in the kitchen to make lunches for the next day and the boys went into Lloyd's bedroom to play.

Gabby stuck the kettle on and made Carl a cup of tea and shouted to him to come and get it. He came out of his workshop and was grateful for the break. They discussed what they were going to do for tea later in the evening and Gabby took her tea into the lounge and sat down with her laptop to get some work done. She wanted to get through some of Isabelle's book before having to go back to the spinal unit.

She was working through the book and found it really interesting. Isabelle had been very talented and had a glittering career. The book was totally different to what she was used to proofreading but she was really enjoying the change. It was great to learn about this lady's life.

The boys came in the room whilst she was working and wanted some snacks so she gave them a drink and a packet of crisps to keep them going until tea time.

That night, Gabby had repacked her bag ready for her next trip to the spinal unit and was sat in bed with her laptop trying to keep up with her emails regarding books that needed proofreading.

She was really pleased with how her life of proofreading was going. This was something really positive for her. She was so grateful each day for this work coming into her life. Her love of books was very similar to her love of horses and it felt good to be working on them for her way of life just like she had previously been doing when she was working with horses.

The alarm went off the next morning early and she got up and made her way to the harbour to go back to England for her new trip to the spinal unit. It was a nice dry day, not a breath of wind, so it was going to be a good journey over. Gabby checked in at the harbour and then sat waiting in the queue of cars to get onto the ferry. There were lots of cars lined up that day waiting to get on and a huge amount of motorbikes. There must have been some event going on somewhere that they were all going to.
As she was waiting there, she could see the ferry and cars started coming off. It wouldn't be long now until she was able to get on. Gabby hated the waiting around, she just wanted to get on, parked up and in her seat ready to leave. She didn't have long to wait and the ferry ground crew were telling them to start going on the ferry. She drove slowly on the boat with her hazard lights flashing so they knew she would need assistance.

She drove to the right-hand side and up the
ramp. She was directed to go round the end of
the ship and turn and up the middle to the front
and then told to park. She got her things
together and started getting her chair out of the
car. She grabbed a big scarf she was going to
take with her to keep warm and her bag with her
essentials and her Kindle so she could spend her
time reading to pass the time.

She made her way across the boat to the lift to
find her way to her seat. She was taken up in the
lift and went round to find her seat. She sat in a
large space that had plenty of room for her chair
so she put her brakes on and set her stuff on the
table and got sat down ready to work. She liked
that position on the boat as it meant she could
relax and have a table to lean her stuff on and
she could also sit and people watch if she felt
like it.

The journey was four long hours. They pulled in
to the harbour and an announcement on the
tannoy was asking all car drivers to get in their
cars. She picked up all her belongings and made
her way to the lift. After getting down in the lift,
she found her car was blocked in so she had to
wait until some of the cars moved to allow her to
get to her car and get in. She finally got into her
car and got herself sorted for the journey to the
unit for her next sessions.

She drove off the boat and headed to the unit. She was staying at the hospital accommodation, which was basic but clean and it just meant she could park up and not have to go anywhere else until she had finished her time there.

CHAPTER 59

She got to the unit after a three-hour drive and went to collect her key to the room she was staying in, dumped her bags in the room and went down to the cafe to get herself a drink. She was feeling pretty tired out and thought she'd sit down with a drink and check on her emails and work out what needed to be done work-wise then, hopefully she'd feel more refreshed ready to go and do a session on the callipers.

She ordered a coffee and sat down at a table, sent messages to Carl and Lloyd to let them know she'd reached the spinal unit and checked her emails. Nothing urgent had come in so she closed them and sat back in her chair to drink her coffee.

As she was drinking, she heard a familiar voice. She looked over and saw Rose pushing towards her. She looked a lot better in herself. She came over to speak to Gabby and gave her a hug. She said she was going to grab a drink and bring it over to join her if that was okay. Gabby told her it was absolutely fine. She quickly came over and sat with Gabby at the table.

'So, how are things?' Gabby asked.

Rose said she was doing okay. She'd been getting used to the routine and going along to her physio sessions. She was excited to see Gabby. She wanted to talk to her as she had been getting some movement back and some of her sensations were also returning, so she was thrilled that things were not looking as bleak as they had been when they last spoke.

Gabby was really happy for her. They chatted about what they had planned for her next and Rose said the physios were working on getting the movement back. They were not going to promise anything but from the way things were going for her she could well be back on her feet when leaving the hospital. Gabby could not have been more happy for her. She was so pleased to see what had been a frightened, somewhat broken young girl sat now in front of her with such positivity and optimism for the future. It was really great news.

They both finished off their drinks and left the cafe together. Rose had physio and Gabby was going there to work on her callipers so she pushed along with her. It was truly like speaking to a totally different person.

As they got to the door to go in, Rose said to Gabby, 'I couldn't have done this without the chat we had. You kept me going and I want to thank you.'

Gabby was quite surprised but happy that she had been able to make a difference. She told Rose she was very welcome and she'd always be on the end of a phone if she needed to talk. They then went into the physio and went off in their separate directions.

Gabby got her callipers out of the cupboard and pushed over to the bars. She put them on and stood up in the bars. There was a mirror in front of her and she stood for a moment looking at herself standing there, finding it hard to remember how it had been to just walk up to a mirror when her legs worked as they were designed to do. It was strange how quickly those things become hard to remember.

Gabby did a good hour going up and down the bars. She could feel she was so much stronger than when she first put the callipers on and felt like she was all stiff and awkward. She wasn't freaking out about falling all the time and she could feel her core was so much stronger, and she looked better too.

She got down after the session and was tired but happy that she was working hard on keeping her body strong.

She took the callipers back into the cupboard, left the physio and made her way back to her room.

CHAPTER 60

Back in her room, she put the kettle on and switched the television on for some background noise. It always felt less lonely when there were other voices in the room. She messaged both Carl and Lloyd to tell them how she got on and ask how their days had been. Switching on her laptop, she transferred onto the bed, took her drink over and ran through her emails.

She had a few new books come in that would be due in the next few weeks so she sent her replies to them and put them in her calendar in the order she needed to do them by and then she saw she'd had an email from Isabelle. She opened the email and Isabelle had said she thought she'd drop her a line to see if she would like to come over to America and meet whilst she was working on the book. Gabby had never been asked to meet an author like this before but the thought was appealing. They could all do with getting some sun. The rest of the email from Isabelle said that she had plenty of room in her house for them all to stay with her if they came over. They would love to show them around and she could get a better feel of what her life was like.

She'd like to show Gabby some of the places that she mentioned. She had lots of photos she'd like to share with her which, due to the volume, wouldn't be in the book, but she wanted to share them with her. The final sentences totally threw Gabby. It said, 'Of course as this is us inviting you. We will pay for all your travel, that includes you and your husband and son, and we won't take no for an answer. Just let us know when you can all get away and we will send the tickets. We will be at the airport to meet you when you arrive in America.' Gabby stared at the email not, believing what she had just read. This was such a great offer but could they really accept something so generous? Especially as Isabelle would also be paying her for her work on her book. This was something she needed to speak to Carl about. She decided this was definitely not something that could be done via messages or email, so she gave him a call. Carl answered after the third ring and was surprised to hear from Gabby. She quickly said that nothing was wrong but something wonderful had come through via email and she wanted them both to know about it as soon as possible. She went through the email and he didn't say a thing until she finished telling him what the email had said. Then she stopped and said, 'So what do you think?'

The phone went quiet for a moment and then he said, 'Why not, I'm up for it if you are and half-term is coming up.'

So, between the two of them, they decided that she'd get back to Isabelle and tell them they would love to accept her wonderfully kind offer and could they go over for the next half-term. She sent the email and sat back. A feeling of excitement came over her. She was stunned at the generosity of someone she had never met. This was something that she thought only ever happened in films.

CHAPTER 61

The next few days, she worked on Isabelle's book and spent two hours a day in the physio on the callipers. She also went to some of the lectures the newly injured patients were having for them to be able to ask her questions if they had any. It was something she herself had hated when she was injured but now that she had been going through life, she appreciated that there were some that would want to know how things are in life, and would want to ask different questions. She was happy to answer any question they wanted to ask.

That day she was asked about clothing and what kind of clothing could they wear now and did any kind of clothes cause problems. They also asked about getting around and working. Some of the injured patients needed to get back to work but like her, they were in jobs previously that they would no longer be able to do now, so she talked to them about what they could do and gave them advice from what she had done for herself. The lecture finished and she left for the day and went back to her room. She needed to get on with some of her work and catch up with Carl and Lloyd.

Lloyd would have finished school by now, so she was going to do a video chat so she could see them both whilst they chatted. She rang as soon as she got in her room and they answered straight away. Lloyd had been doing his homework but was happy to stop to chat. They all said how nice it was to see each other and Carl told her he had filled Lloyd in about the trip to America and he was super excited. They chatted about what they'd all been doing and Gabby said she'd check her email during their conversation as she had her laptop next to her. Waiting in her inbox was an email from Isabelle. She said they were both thrilled to bits that they had said yes to the offer to come and visit. They bought the tickets for them and they were attached to the email.

They lived in Clearwater, Florida so the plane from England would take them to Tampa and then the driver would take them from the airport to Clearwater, where they would both be waiting on their arrival rather than them hanging around in the arrivals for them. Gabby finished reading the email and Lloyd shouted 'yippee' down the phone and they all started chatting excitedly about what they would see out there. They all wanted to go online to see what Clearwater looked like. This was going to be a special holiday. It was like being VIPs, not having to pay for things.

It made them all feel a bit awkward but when they talked about it, they tried to put that into the back of their minds, remembering what Isabelle had said to her to think of it as background to the proofreading and forget about them treating them. They all sat and chatted about it and how it was only a matter of weeks and they would be able to enjoy some sunshine. They ended the call and said they'd all catch up again tomorrow.

Gabby replied to the email from Isabelle thanking her very much again for this holiday and telling her how much they were all looking forward to meeting them both.

CHAPTER 62

That evening, she went online and had a look at what Clearwater was like. It looked beautiful. A really pretty town and the cleanest, white sandy beach she had ever seen, and huge posh houses lining the streets, it looked like the most beautiful place she had ever seen. It felt strange to think that in just two weeks they would be in that place and they would be able to view these landmarks for real.

Gabby got herself ready for bed and got her headphones and phone out. She chose a meditation to put her in a relaxed state ready for bed. This was her nightly routine now and if she skipped it, she really felt the difference the next day. This was something she did for her own health and wellbeing.

She listened that night to a calming mindfulness meditation. She then wrote in her journals; the gratitude journal, the daily journal, and her future diary. She found that just writing things down got all worries out of her mind and her gratitude diary helped to remind her about all the things she had in her life that she had to be grateful for.

That night, Gabby went to bed dreaming of the trip ahead.

The following day started with Gabby working on her proofreading; she spent two hours going through the books she was working on. She wanted to leave part of Isabelle's book for nearer the trip so she could discuss the events with Isabelle when they were there. She was also working on a fictional book that was a romance. It was easy reading and Gabby was happily working her way through each page, methodically working her way through each line.

She was finding out that even after the books had been edited, there was always still so much she could uncover that needed amending and it was a really satisfying job. She loved being part of helping someone get their book out and published. She was only a small cog in the grand scheme of the book becoming published and out there for sale but she took pride in the part she had in it.

Her phone rang and she clicked on save and then answered it. It was Isabelle. She was asking Gabby if she knew exactly what her husband did for a living. Gabby said she only knew what was in the book.

Isabelle explained that her husband was working on ways to get spinal injured people back on their feet. Gabby said that's what she had gathered from the book. Isabelle said to her, 'John wants to know if you'd like to be part of his study.' Gabby was stunned. She did not know what to say. She had not seen that coming. It was a huge thing to be asked. She didn't say anything for a moment and Isabelle asked her if she was still on the line. Gabby answered saying yes, she was just taking it in. She told her that she'd need to speak to Carl as this was something that would affect them all. Isabelle said to take as much time as she needs. That John said if she wanted to go ahead, he would make sure he gave her all the information and she could ask as many questions as she wanted to when they saw them during half-term. Gabby got off the phone and was again in shock. She called her home number straight away and told Carl what had just happened and asked him what he thought. He too was shocked but said it was definitely something they should consider as long as there were minimal risks, as he didn't want anything else to happen to make her mobility worse, and she totally agreed.

CHAPTER 63

With all the things that were happening for her, she was thinking this is the universe giving her back all the good things she'd been giving out. She was receiving lots of opportunities with her work on the books, then the trip to meet the author and her husband and to top it off, the offer of being part of this new treatment. She was so overjoyed with the things that were coming their way. Working on the way she thought about things, helping others and always being mindful of how her actions could make others feel. On top of that, her daily chats to her angels were also something that helped keep her in a positive mindset and helped curb any negative thoughts before they started to take over thoughts and attract more negativity. Gabby always thought that she wished she had known about angels and how much they can help you many years ago as life could have been so different, but she also realised that she had to go through the things that had happened to her to appreciate the way things had changed for her with her being able to help others and her family and the success of her business.

She knew that this had come from having help from her angels and wished that everyone could make the most of the angels that are there for them. Our angels are with us all the time and twiddling their thumbs waiting and hoping to be asked to be part of our lives and for us to ask for help. They want to help us but they won't do this if you don't ask. When you first start working with your angels, this is something you often forget to do and then wonder why things haven't changed. You always have to remember to believe, trust and most importantly ask for help. It is like opening a door to all you've dreamed of. They will not help if you ask for something that would cause ill will or hurt to others but if you are asking for something that is for the greater good then you can ask for as much as you want. They will do their best to help. You may not know how it will manifest to you but it will come to you in the best way. You have to be patient.

These things are not always instant and sometimes they may feel like it isn't the right time for this thing to happen, so you may have to wait until they believe the time is right.

CHAPTER 64

The next couple of hours were spent in the physio on her callipers. She was in deep thought that day going up and down the rails. She stood still looking at herself in the mirror and thinking about the conversation she'd had with Isabelle. Could this work? Could she be walking without these restricting callipers and using her legs like they used to all those years ago – and it really was a long time ago. One of the physios came over to her and asked if she was okay as she was just standing there and she was worried something was wrong. She turned to the physio and said, 'Quite the opposite, actually,' and explained what had been going on. The physio was really interested to learn about what the treatment was and Gabby said she would tell her all she found out when they come back from America. But for now, she said she was continuing to concentrate on keeping her body healthy. She finished her calliper session and went back to the cupboard to put them away. Then off she went to the lecture room to get to the next session for the patients' learning.

The session was on bladder and bowel management. Not the nicest discussion to have but she knew it was important, so was happy to sit and be there for any questions. The patients all sat in the session in silence. None of them looked like they wanted to be there and they were not like the last lot asking questions all the way through. She knew it was a tough subject to hear and when you first hear what the lecturer says you feel like shouting at her as she is able-bodied and doesn't have to cope with the things she is talking about. She stood there telling them what could happen if they didn't drink enough and what could happen if they didn't empty their bowels properly, and she didn't hold back on the details. The looks on the patients faces at the end was sheer horror.

Gabby really felt for them and knew how they were all feeling. She knew they were scared for the future and that they wondered what would happen if they didn't do it right or if something went wrong. Gabby told them all that even though it seemed terrifying right now and it really was a serious subject. But she wanted to reassure them that this was something they would be taught to manage and they weren't going to be just left to figure it out.

She told them the spinal unit is so strict with patients; they don't allow anyone out of the hospital until they are confident they have the knowledge to look after their well-being and that they also have the right mind-set, so that if there is an issue, they know that they will contact the hospital and ask for help, or go to the hospital and talk about it to them and not just ignore it and hope it goes away.

After this, there were a few faces not looking quite so worried but a couple still looked really upset. She said to them that she felt just the way they did and found it all too much to take in, but they will get there, and if they wanted to ask her any more questions, they would no doubt see her around the hospital and were welcome to just come and ask.

At the end of the day, Gabby went back to her room and decided on just having a bowl of cereal for tea. She'd had a decent lunch earlier on and she was still feeling pretty full. She went to her room and got herself comfortable. She contacted Carl and Lloyd to ask how their days had been and said she'd see if she could find out what things they could possibly see when they go to Clearwater. Lloyd said he'd mentioned it at school and lots of people had said they had heard of it but never been.

Carl said he'd been on the internet looking at pictures and it looked like an amazing place to go, so thought they were really lucky to get this chance.

The next two days went by in a flash, going into physio and working on her callipers, then going to the lectures. She also had four new patients who had come into the hospital to visit. She just went and introduced herself and offered to help or just chat with them, and said if they wanted anyone to talk to her, that they could ask any questions and she'd do her best to answer them all.

She also went to see how Rose was getting on. She was like a new person; she had so much more of her confidence back. It was an amazing transformation from when they first met. She had started to get more movement back and was now able to stand by herself. Her walking was also starting but she was still needing help at the moment. It was coming back and the future looked really good for her. It was an excellent outcome and not one you see very often in the spinal unit. Not often enough anyway from Gabby's point of view.

CHAPTER 65

She was now back on the ferry on her way home again. These trips were tiring but she knew that she was making a difference to herself and to other people. And Carl and Lloyd were happy that she was getting her wellbeing back on track. It had been a long time coming, but after she discovered the way of thinking positively, things began to change, so she would do more and more of it, and more positive things came her way. This was how she was living her life now and it was a change for the better.

That month, she had set the intention to have money coming to her easily and for her to walk again. The money was coming in already, the proofreading was going from strength to strength and now the author had invited them to America and offered her to be part of a trial. This could be her manifestation coming into reality for her.

She would always ask for something and if it was the right time it would happen, but if the universe and angels didn't believe she was ready, then something else would turn up for her to learn from, and it would be because they didn't believe she was ready yet.

Gabby had a good feeling about this trip though. She spoke constantly to her angels and they knew everything. She sometimes wondered if she gave them headaches for talking to them too much, but she knew they were always happy to listen and they probably found Gabby's conversations funny at times.

The ferry was bumpy this time and there were lots of clattering cups and bottles. She thought she'd just stay firmly in her seat and not attempt to move anywhere in case she fell. So she got her book out and read for a bit, then just sat back and relaxed and tried to look out the window and ignore the sounds of people being ill in the background. The ferry arrived at the Island on time and she was again the last to get off because her car was blocked in. She drove back to the house and found Carl and Lloyd still having their tea. She pushed in and put some of her bags down, went outside and got the rest, then sat with them whilst they finished eating. She was glad to be back on dry land after all the rocking around. It wasn't a pleasant feeling and she sometimes felt that it was never-ending.

The next few weeks went flying by and before they all knew it, they were packing for their trip to America.

They had to catch the earliest flight off the Island the next morning so they were all eager to get an early night.

They went through all their checklists but didn't have to take nearly as much as they would have if they were going alone. They would be taken around by Isabelle and John, so they didn't need to hire a car and wouldn't need to take their sat nav. This was going to be a totally new experience. And also, a bit strange in one way because they had never met and it all came about with Gabby working with Isabelle on her book. It was something Gabby was looking forward to though. She never normally got to speak face-to-face with the authors whilst working on their books, so this would be fun to be able to ask her things literally as it happened. Gabby got Lloyd off to bed that night and read him a story. He had taken his travel pill and was all set for the adventure they would all be going on the next day. She kissed him goodnight and told him to try to go straight to sleep as it would be a busy day the next day. She went out of his room and closed the door.

Carl called her and asked if she'd checked all her toiletries and if she'd got all her tablets sorted. Gabby said she had, but having been asked, she then felt she needed to check yet again. She knew her memory was like a sieve at times, so went back into the bedroom to recheck everything she had already gone through.

All her catheters were correct and she had spares in case they got delayed. She also had more than enough tablets for exactly the same reason. She had copies of her prescriptions in case there were any questions about the medications she was carrying. This hadn't happened so far but she always took them in the hope it still would not happen.

She didn't sleep well at all that night for fear of oversleeping and missing the plane. The alarm went off at 4.30am and they were all wandering around like zombies getting ready to get off to the airport. They left the house and had a taxi waiting for them as they didn't want to leave their car in the airport for two weeks' worth of parking.

The road was clear going to the airport; most people were still in their beds with no thoughts of getting up. They got to the airport in record time; the taxi driver seemed to be in a hurry and drove like he was in New York. They thought that if he did get caught by the police for speeding please let it be after he had safely dropped them off.

They got out of the car and thanked him and paid him and he shot off like a getaway driver. Clearly, he had somewhere he needed to be. They checked in and handed over their suitcases, then headed towards the queue waiting to get through the scanner.

Every time, Gabby went anywhere she got searched. No matter where she was going or who she was with. So, she was fully prepared. Some airports were more thorough than others though. She often wondered in all her years of being in a chair, why had not one person in the airport actually checked the cushion she was sitting on. Her cushion had silicone at the back of it to help prevent pressure sores and although she knew she would never take anything into the plane that shouldn't be on it, she was scared at the thought that someone could use that as a way of taking something on one day. The cushion was even taken onto the plane with her and kept in the overhead locker but it was the one thing that had never been through the scanner.

Gabby wasn't a good flyer so thoughts like this always went through her mind during the journey and she was far too scared to truly relax. The slightest bit of turbulence sent her into a panic and she was praying like mad. This time she had downloaded a new meditation for people who were scared of flying, so when they got in the air for the London to Tampa flight, she was going to put it on and see if she could manage to relax at all.

The Island flight to London went smoothly.

They were no sooner up in the air and offered a drink, when the crew came round taking the cups back off them ready to tidy up for landing. Gabby was saying positive affirmations to herself in her head to keep the feeling of calm. They got off the plane and were taken in a minibus to the other side of the airport for their connecting flight. When they checked in to the flight, they were taken into a different part of the airport they hadn't been in before and they were all looking at each other wondering where they were going. The ground crew said the plane would be ready to take off in about thirty minutes and someone would come and get them when it was time to make their way to the plane. So they got settled and Carl went and got a drink for himself and Lloyd. Gabby was too nervous to have a drink. She was already working out how many times she would need to get into a small aisle chair and into the toilet whilst on the plane and she thought if she didn't drink too much perhaps she could make it just twice in the journey. She knew that it was a silly thing to do and that you were told to keep hydrated, but going to the toilet on the plane and pushing past people to get to it when being dragged backwards in the aisle chair was humiliating.

She was glad the patients at the hospital hadn't asked her any questions on coping with flying and toilet breaks on the plane.
How on Earth would she respond to those without sounding negative?

CHAPTER 66

As Carl was walking back to them with his drink, a man came over to them and said, 'We are ready for you now.'

They were surprised as they hadn't heard anything announced on the tannoy, but got their things together and followed the man. As they were going through the corridors, there didn't appear to be many people going the same way, but Gabby just took it that it was because they had a wheelchair with them so it was a way to the plane with less traffic. She couldn't have been more wrong. They got to a door with a pin code access. The man typed in his number and let them through. They were the only ones in their little room. There was a lady waiting for them in there and said, 'Hey, you must be Gabby, Carl and Lloyd. I'm Tiffany and I'm going to be looking after you on your flight, do you want to follow me?'

They all said a quiet hello back and followed Tiffany. She led them outside and what was in front of them was a huge private plane. They stopped and couldn't believe what was happening.

Gabby said, 'Excuse me Tiffany, are we going on that plane?'

Tiffany replied, 'Yes, of course. This is John's plane. Did you not know?' Gabby told her no they had just assumed it would be a normal flight to America, not for one minute did they think of being on a private plane. They had never travelled business class, let alone first class and now, they were about to get on a private jet, where they would be travelling in luxury all the way to America. Gabby was so incredibly grateful and couldn't wait to give Isabelle and John a huge hug of thanks. This made her feel somewhat less nervous as she wouldn't need to worry about bothering other people as she brushed past them to the toilet. Inside the plane, it was massive. They had a big toilet where Gabby had plenty of room to move around and the chair on board the plane was a bit bigger than a normal aisle chair so she was able to get to the toilet by herself and not have to ask for help each time, which was a major advantage. They all had beds to get on and their own televisions and spaces for laptops or iPads, whichever they wanted, and lots of nice toiletries to keep them comfortable. They were also given drinks and food before allowing them the time to relax and settle in.

There was time for them all to have a sleep if they felt the need or to just lie back, relax and enjoy the flight.

Gabby knew what she was doing straight away. She made sure Lloyd was happy with how things were in his section. He was thrilled with where he was; he had children's films, games and sweets galore. He said he might have a sleep in a bit but was going to play for a while. Carl was happy to sit and watch a film and take in all the gadgets they had on board and was impressed at the services and equipment they had in there with them.

So, Gabby wished them both a good night, popped to the toilet, got herself ready and then transferred onto the bed. It was so comfortable and was such a luxury being able to actually have your legs up whilst flying. She put on her eye mask and listened to her meditation before drifting off to sleep.

She was woken up by Tiffany telling her they would be coming in to land in about thirty minutes and asking if she'd had a good sleep. Gabby could not believe how long she had slept. She was amazed. She didn't sleep that well at home. Perhaps, it was the meditation. Either way, she was feeling wonderfully relaxed and refreshed. She looked over to Carl and Lloyd. They too had just been woken up and were also feeling happy and they both said they slept really well.

They all got themselves ready to get off the plane. They were given some breakfast and to Lloyd's delight, they gave him a pain au chocolat. One happy boy. By the time the breakfast things had been taken away, the plane was approaching the runway. They all sat waiting to land. The plane gently came down to the ground and they had the smoothest landing they'd ever felt. Gabby looked out of the window and still couldn't quite believe they were in a plane without loads of other people. The plane came to a standstill and they got their things together. Tiffany helped them all off the plane and took them through to customs. They didn't even have to queue; they went straight into a special part of the airport for private planes. This was the height of luxury.

CHAPTER 67

As they moved through customs and took the
luggage through, they were taken to a waiting
vehicle. The driver was really cheerful. He asked
how their journey had been and took all their
luggage, popped it in the boot, and they all got
in. The driver was also very chatty and was
telling them about the areas they were passing.
There was so much space over there. Land as far
as the eye could see and the sun was out and
showing everything looking beautiful.
They drove along a very fast main road that had
many lanes; they were zipping in and out of the
lanes and it was a strange feeling to be
undercutting people. They had quite a long
drive to reach Clearwater. Turning off the main
road, they drove into a more built-up area and
on reaching this area, there were shops and
houses. The houses looked very different to back
home. There were lots of wooden-looking
houses in huge plots of land and the shops
looked like farm shops. They continued down
the road and the scenery changed again. They
were coming into an area that was obviously
where the money was.

The houses were huge, and some had big gates out the front.

The driver said to them, 'Welcome to Clearwater.'

Driving by, they looked at beautiful houses with gardens that looked spotless and lots of lovely-looking places to go for dinner along the road going through Clearwater. There were shops that were selling beach balls and stuff for taking on the beach, and tourist shops. They drove a little way and the driver said to them, 'I'm just going to stop over here and show you something before we carry on to the house.'

He pulled on a slip road and Carl and Lloyd jumped out of the car. Carl grabbed Gabby's wheelchair and she got out. They walked along the slipway and what they saw was magical, the most amazing, white, pristine beach they had ever seen. It was huge; it looked even more beautiful than what they had seen on the internet. They turned to look at the driver and he said, 'That was worth the stop, wasn't it?' They all agreed and turned back to get back in the car. Back on the road, they were all feeling even more grateful for being there. Lucky didn't come close to how they felt. It was only a short drive from the beach they had stopped at and they pulled up to a long driveway; there were electric gates where the driver spoke into a security device on arrival.

The gates opened and in front of them was a tree-lined drive. They made their way slowly down the drive. The drive opened up into a large turning circle in front of the house with a fountain in the middle. The house was very large and standing at the door waiting for them were two people who Gabby guessed were Isabelle and John.

The couple came over to the car and welcomed them to their home. They showed them inside and took them to their rooms. The house was like something you'd see in a magazine. Gabby was so glad it was dry outside, she wouldn't have wanted to drag wet wheel marks all over the floor. The rooms they had been given were downstairs and they both had ensuite bathrooms. They were very homely and bright. As soon as they got their things settled down in the rooms, they went into the living area and Isabelle had made some drinks for them. The three of them sat down and they all started to chat. Isabelle and John also had a son, Milo, who was slightly older than Lloyd but he spoke to Lloyd and asked if he'd like to see his room. He wanted to show him the games room they have. Lloyd was so happy to see he would have someone to play with. He happily went off with his new friend.

Gabby was eager to talk to Isabelle about how the book was going and mentioned some of the things she'd read so far and Isabelle gave her lots more information about what she'd done with her life. It sounded like something dreams are made of. What a life this lady had experienced. It was such an interesting job learning about how people live; so many different lives on one Earth.

She spoke for some time on her life and got pictures out to show Gabby. John was showing Carl around the house and the outside area.

CHAPTER 68

Isabelle said to Gabby that the main reason they asked them over was to tell them about what John was working on. She said he had been working on ways to help people with spinal cord injuries for years, but now they were at the stage where they could safely insert the electrode into patients. He had spoken to Isabelle about Gabby and asked her if she thought that Gabby would like to be a part of this trial. Gabby said to Isabelle that it was something she had always put out there that she wanted to walk again someday. She'd never ever walked with Carl and Lloyd and would love more than anything to be able to go out on fields and beaches walking with them. Or just walking to the shop.

It would be lovely to not have the need to plan where you go all the time in case when you get there the wheelchair couldn't go in. She told Isabelle she was excited about the fact she was being given this opportunity. She said that a lot of people she knew from being in the spinal unit would love to be in her position, so she was going to make the most of the chance they had given her.

They discussed other things after that. They found out that they both loved to meditate, both of them believed in angels and were mad about crystals. Isabelle got loads of crystals out to show Gabby and they were still looking at them when John and Carl came back in the room from their tour of the grounds.

Both men looked at each other and said, 'Uh oh, once they start on crystals there is no stopping them.'

They sat down and Isabelle said to John, 'Why don't you tell Gabby a bit more about what you are doing?'

He told Gabby the implant would be placed below the level of her injury and it stimulates the nervous tissue that is still connected to the leg muscles.

He said he would have to put the implant in and then they would see how her body reacts. He told her everyone would be different as all of the spinal injuries are so very different. He said that she wouldn't be at risk; that he could do the operation and she would only have a short stay in the hospital. She wouldn't have to have many stitches as the electrode would be quite small.

He said he would make sure she had a nice neat scar and it would disappear quite quickly. That was the last thing Gabby was worried about. She asked what would happen next.

Would they have to travel back in a few months, or how would this work?

He said with her permission that she could have it done whilst they were there. He said if she signed forms he could get medical details from the spinal unit in the UK and then he would need to do some tests, but if they were happy he could get things moving as soon as possible.

Gabby looked at Carl in shock. She was totally not expecting that. She thought that they would be having a holiday, not a hospital stay. This was the moment the boys walked in.

Lloyd saw Gabby's face and said, 'Mummy, what's wrong?'

She told him what they had been talking about and he looked scared. She said to him, 'It's okay.'

It was what they had talked about at home and although they hadn't expected it for some months at least, this way they didn't get the chance to sit and worry for weeks on end.

So, Lloyd gave her a big hug and said, 'As long as you are going to be okay.'

She looked at John and he said to Lloyd, 'Don't worry, Lloyd. I will take good care of Mummy for you.'

Lloyd smiled but didn't seem too confident and stayed by Gabby's side. She knew it was going to be really hard on him and Carl.

CHAPTER 69

After dinner that evening, they all went to bed and it was nice to be in a proper bed. Despite having a great sleep on the plane, they were all very tired. Before going off to sleep, Gabby spoke to Carl about the treatment. She said that she was shocked that it was going to be happening whilst they were there and asked if he minded after them thinking it was going to be a holiday.

He said no, he didn't mind, and that it still would be a holiday. She wouldn't be in the hospital for very long and what better place to recover than in this beautiful setting with the warm weather on top, which would surely help aid the process. She agreed and they both went off to sleep.

They woke to the sound of the birds and the sun shone through the windows even though the curtains were closed. Gabby got out of bed and looked outside. It was glorious, the sky was as blue as could be and there was not a cloud to be seen. She thought back to their friends and knew they would be saying that it's perfect conditions for skydiving.

Carl sat up and said he wondered what the day was going to be like for them all. Lloyd came walking in, already dressed. He'd been playing with Milo. They were keen to get on playing with each other again after the fun they'd had the previous day. Lloyd asked Gabby and Carl if it was okay for him to go in the pool with Milo and they both said yes as long as they were sensible. They both said they'd be fine and went off to get changed into their swimming things. Gabby and Carl got dressed and went into the room they had been in the night before and Isabelle called for them to come through. They followed the sound of her voice and she was in the kitchen making breakfast. From the kitchen, you could see straight out to the pool, which was a relief for Gabby as she had wanted to keep an eye on the boys whilst they were playing in the pool. Isabelle said they could take breakfast outside with it being so warm, so Carl helped to carry everything out and they all sat at a table and ate and chatted and watched the boys laughing and playing.

Isabelle said John had gone off to his hospital early and was getting all things prepared for taking Gabby in to do her operation. Gabby's stomach lurched; the word operation made her feel sick. She thought perhaps if you called it a procedure it didn't sound half as scary.

She didn't eat much more after that, thinking about the imminent procedure. What was it going to be like? It had been twenty-three years since she could walk. Would she get it back? What if it didn't work? Would she still be in a lot of pain after? Talking to John about it, he'd said they didn't want to confirm any of the things she may get back until they tried it as there had been varying success stories, but as the injuries were all unique he didn't want to make a promise and for it not to come true.

Sitting outside in the warmth and just relaxing felt lovely. The warmth on her skin was just what she'd needed after the damp and cold weather they had been having. They were interrupted by the phone ringing and Isabelle went to get it. She stood in the kitchen talking and then came outside with the phone.

They could hear her saying, 'Yes, I'm sure today will be okay. I'll ask and we'll see you in about an hour.'

She ended the conversation and looked at Gabby. 'That was John,' she said. 'He wants to do it today, so that you can have a really good rest after.'

They looked at each other and Gabby said, 'Oh, okay.'

Isabelle said, 'We leave in an hour,' and shouted to the boys that they had half an hour left, then would need to get out and dry as they were going out. Gabby was stunned, this was all going so fast. She really wanted to walk and stand but she was also feeling terribly worried. She asked if anyone would mind if she went in the bedroom by herself for a bit and they all said, 'Not at all.'

It was obvious to them that she needed a moment to take in what was going to be happening. She got in the room and grabbed her headphones. She put them on and transferred onto the bed. She needed to meditate to calm herself and focus on positive thoughts before negativity took hold. She chose a nice spiritual one she had that she used often and sat back and relaxed. This meditation took 30 mins, but after she felt so much better and got up off the bed, put some clothes together and went to join the others. They looked at her and asked if she felt better now and she said, 'Much.'

They were all pretty-much ready to leave. They were just waiting for the boys to get into dry clothes then they'd make a move. Gabby went into the bedroom and grabbed the bag; she wasn't sure how much she'd need so she just took a few clothes and toiletries.

CHAPTER 70

The hospital was about a thirty-minute drive from the house and it looked brand new. Isabelle went into the staff car park and parked next to John's car. They all got out and went in to meet him. John came out of the room he was in and greeted them with a big smile.

He said, 'Come and meet the team.'

So, they all followed him and he introduced them to all the people who would be doing the operation and to the other scientists who were working on this treatment.

Carl was interested to see what the electrode was like so they chatted to him about how it would go in and what the possibilities could mean for Gabby, but she didn't want to see it or hear that bit so she left the room.

Lloyd was looking worried and wanted to stand as close to Gabby as possible. He kept asking her if she'd be okay and she kept telling him, of course, there was nothing for him to worry about. Any operation had risks but this wasn't the time to say that to him. She gave him a big hug and he held on to her for some time.

They heard John saying, 'Sorry to interrupt, but is the patient ready?'

That was Gabby's cue to get herself undressed and off to the theatre. She hugged and kissed Carl and Lloyd and they said they would be there when she woke up.

They went in opposite directions now and Gabby suddenly felt quite worried. She told John she had eaten something that morning but after his phone call, she hadn't been able to eat as she'd been worried that he couldn't do the operation.

He said he knew what she'd had as he had asked Isabelle. He said the operation would be fine to go ahead. Gabby went to use the toilet and got out of her clothes and transferred to the waiting bed. The doctors then put a wristband on her arm and took blood, checked her blood pressure and temperature, and marked her back where they would be cutting.

As they were doing their jobs, Gabby felt a sudden calm come over her. She knew then that her angels were giving her a sign that they were there, they wouldn't leave her, and she was going to be okay. She relaxed at that thought and wondered how she ever lived without speaking to her angels and how she ever got by each day without their help. She wondered how other people got by in life without ever knowing the help they could have if they only became open to it. It had certainly changed her life.

John's voice made her jump, saying they were ready to go and asking if she was okay.

She apologised for being somewhere else for a moment and said she was all set. The bed started to move and she was taken into the theatre. They told her they would be putting her to sleep and then she'd have a nice rest whilst they put the electrode in. She said okay and in a desperate last-minute panic said, 'Please make sure I wake up.' John said, 'Don't worry, we have the very best people and equipment here, you'll be fine.' The needle was put in her arm and she got the horrible feeling of being knocked out.

CHAPTER 71

It took just under two hours to place the spinal cord stimulator wire and subcutaneous pulse generator into Gabby. She woke soon after in the recovery room, feeling very sleepy and thirsty. Carl was in a gown and was allowed to come in and see her. He asked her how she felt and she said she was fine so far.

He said Lloyd was okay; he'd been upset but now he knew she was awake, he was happy and couldn't wait until he was allowed to see her. The nurse came over to check her and gave her a sip of water. She said Gabby would have to stay there for a bit longer, but as soon as the doctor gave the go-ahead, she could go into a room and then she'd be able to see Lloyd.

Gabby was still not quite aware of what was going on and just drifted in and out of sleep for a while and then when she woke, she was in a private room with Carl and Lloyd sat staring at her. She said 'Hello' and Lloyd jumped up to hug her, but remembering she'd had an operation, he gave her a gentle touch on her arms and a kiss on the cheek.

He whispered, 'Love you. I'm glad you're awake.'

She felt a tear come in her eye. Carl was watching and had to swallow back a tear himself. He came over and said, 'Welcome back.' He kissed her and sat back down. He told her John had said the operation went really well and there were no complications. She was just needing to rest and then recover and see how things progressed.

She was only going to stay in the hospital for a couple of nights so they could keep an eye on her wound and blood pressure. As they would be staying with John, they knew he would be taking her straight back in if anything happened. She was so grateful. When John had said he did the research she hadn't realised he was going to do the actual operation. Carl said he didn't know the surgeon was in the theatre and John had to be there too to make sure the equipment got put in properly.

She said to Carl, 'I really feel like a cup of tea right now.'

And he said, 'Coming right up.' He went off to find her a cup of tea.

Lloyd sat telling her what they'd been doing whilst she was asleep. Apparently, John had a cool office where they got to play games, so the boys were playing Fortnite for most of the time she was in theatre.

She was happy hearing this as she hated the thought of him sat there worrying about her. She was starting to feel a lot more alert now and Carl walked in with a drink for her.

He said, 'It is tea but whether it tastes as it does at home, who knows.'

She took it gratefully and tried to sit up. As she did though, she felt pain – gosh, she'd nearly forgotten – so she decided to lie on her side and drink it with a straw for now, to save the discomfort. The nurse asked her if she wanted painkillers and she said, 'No thank you. It only hurts if I move.' Carl rolled his eyes. The tea wasn't what she was used to but she drank all of it; it was so good to have something. She felt dehydrated and the sugar in it helped too. She found it funny how whenever someone gets you a drink in the hospital, they always put sugar in it.

The door opened and in walked Isabelle with a bag of gifts for her. She said, 'Hey, how are you feeling? I got you some little treats to show you how much we all care.'

Gabby smiled at her and said, 'After all this, you're giving me gifts? This is too much.'

Isabelle said, 'Don't be silly Gabby, you're the guinea pig,' and winked at her. They all laughed.

John came in as they were all laughing and said, 'Well, I'm glad to see the patient is feeling better than the last time we spoke.'

She told him she was feeling fine but sore and thanked him for taking care of her and nearly choked with tears when saying, 'And for making sure I woke up again.'

She managed to swallow down the lump in her throat. He squeezed her hand and said 'Don't mention it. Now for the fun part.'

CHAPTER 72

The next few days in the hospital were spent by having lots of tests and checks to make sure all was going well. Gabby was recovering remarkably quickly and feeling so well. She continued to meditate and informed the nurses that she would be doing it so she was left on her own for the time she was doing it. They said they would leave the window blind open though so they could peek in and still keep an eye on her. She said she was fine with that.

She spoke to the angels and thanked them for being with her and helping her keep up her positive thoughts when she was very close to the negativity washing over her and taking over. She asked them to help her recover and to give her the best possible outcome, whatever that may be for her. This was something they would know in time.

The following morning, Isabelle came in and said, 'Would you like to go home?' – meaning her house. Gabby said, 'Yes please.' She had some help with getting dressed and transferring to her chair.

She was okay when she was off the bed as the transfers were easier on firmer surfaces, so she was okay with using the toilet. She did feel a bit weak, but she had Carl and Lloyd waiting outside the room, so if she had a wobble she knew they'd be there.

John had to stay at the hospital for a while but would be back later on. He said he was sending all the details of what they had done straight to the hospital on the Island so they knew exactly what to expect when she got back. They would keep in constant contact with them and also with the spinal unit who he'd also sent all the information to. He was excited to see how things developed for Gabby and really hoped for a bright outcome for her. They got to the car and Gabby gingerly transferred as it was quite a stretch into the car. Once she was in, she was fine, but felt a bit low as she was not used to needing help to that extent.

The drive back to Clearwater was smooth and they were soon driving up the long drive to the house. Gabby found transferring out of the car was easier than getting in. They all went in and Carl put Gabby's things in their room. Gabby was happy to be home, even if it wasn't their own home. Being away from the medical smells made such a lot of difference for recovering.

They went in the living area and Isabelle said she was going to make a light lunch for everyone so they could sit and relax and put the television on, or if the boys wanted to swim they could go outside and watch. Gabby knew what the answer would be but she still offered to help. She hated the thought of being waited on and not offering to help, to her it felt very rude. Isabelle gave her a look, which, even though they had only met just days ago, she knew it meant 'don't even think about it.'

CHAPTER 73

Carl and Gabby went outside; the boys had decided to swim so they went out to be nearby. Gabby found having the sun on her was a good feeling. She was feeling sore from the journey in the car and thought she could do with a good night's sleep and a relaxing day after to give her back some healing time.

She was wondering how long it would be until she'd know if anything was happening.

Her thoughts were stopped by the boys shouting, 'Look over there,' pointing towards the purple sage plant. Fluttering by it was a hummingbird. These were not something they saw in the UK, so Lloyd was excited to see it. So too were Carl and Gabby. It was beautiful. Watching the bird, Gabby felt so happy and so very grateful to be there.

They were in a house with the most generous family and experiencing new wonderful things. She was wondering how she could ever repay their generosity.

Isabelle came outside. She saw them watching the bird and said, 'Beautiful aren't they?' John came back later in the evening.

He said all paperwork was sent to the two hospitals in the UK and he'd keep them informed of any progress. He said it was good to see she was smiling and looking bright. He said she was to take it easy for a few days then they would take them out and about. They stayed outside; the boys continued to play for hours, in and out of the pool. When it was time for tea the boys got out, put some dry clothes on and they all sat outside with the lights on and ate from the barbeque. They had the most delicious salad Gabby had ever tasted.

It was a fun evening but by 10 pm, Gabby was feeling very tired. She had told Lloyd to get ready for bed earlier and she said to everyone, 'I'm sorry but I'm going to have to call it a night. I'm tired out.' They all said, 'Absolutely.'

She went off and got herself ready for bed. She took her medication and the extra painkillers they had given her at the hospital and got into bed.

She couldn't remember Carl coming in; she was fast asleep as soon as her head hit the pillow. She was so tired. She had the most relaxing night's sleep that night. Carl came in about 11.30 pm and got in bed. He was tired but he'd stayed out and enjoyed some wine with John and Isabelle after the boys had gone to bed.

CHAPTER 74

Gabby woke up early the next morning. She felt wide awake and really well. She was lying in the bed wondering what they would do that day and suddenly felt her left leg move. She looked down and thought, was that real? Then she threw the covers off her legs and watched them, and it happened again, her leg moved.

She nudged Carl and said, 'My legs are moving.' He shot up in bed and watched and she was really moving her legs. Gabby had tears running down her cheeks. She looked at him and said, 'It's happening. This is what my legs were like. I could move them before; I never thought this day would come.' They were now both crying happy tears. It was an amazing moment.

She said to him, 'I think we need to get up and show John.'

So, they chucked some clothes on and went into the kitchen.

John and Isabelle were already up and drinking coffee. Isabelle offered them some and they both said yes please, but Gabby said, 'Please, watch this first.'

Isabelle stopped what she was doing and John walked over. Gabby lifted her legs up as she was sitting there, bending and straightening them. She was beaming and John was looking amazed. He said to her, 'This is fantastic. Are you in any pain? Do you feel okay when this is happening?' Gabby told him no, she felt fine. It was the memory coming back of what it used to feel like, and it felt very overwhelming.

Carl said, 'How does this all work?'

John said he wasn't sure why this stimulation allowed the patient to take control of their legs. It was a possibility that there were some intact nerve fibres capable of transmitting brain signals to her legs. He said that this was Gabby starting to regain voluntary control of her legs.

He went to get his laptop and was taking a note of what had happened and what movement and sensation Gabby was regaining. He asked Gabby if he could examine her legs.

She said yes.

He put his hand on her leg and she was shocked; she shouted, 'I can feel it, I can feel it.'

Lloyd had just got up and ran over asking what had happened. They told him nothing bad. He came over and Gabby showed him how she could now move her legs.

She said, 'Put your hand on my leg.' He did and she said to him, 'Lloyd, I can feel your hand.'

He burst into tears. He said, 'Mummy, I'm so happy.'

That was just the beginning. They decided to stop for now and to have some breakfast and go out for the day seeing as things were changing so much. They were going to stay in but they would be tempted to keep trying things so they thought they'd go into Clearwater and do some tourist stuff.

They all went in the car and John drove into Clearwater. They went into the town. It was lovely. They went in shops that sold t-shirts with Clearwater on and postcards, beach balls and all manner of beach toys, towels, and lots of magnets and trinkets with Clearwater on.

They got some little tourist things to take back with them and then went out to go get a drink. They went to a coffee shop nearby. The boys decided they were hungry so they had big milkshakes with lots of ice-cream and chocolate sprinkles and other sweets. They were huge. They were becoming really good friends. It was lovely for them to see the friendship between the two of them. They were glad that Lloyd was still happy, having fun times with someone of his own age along with everything else that was happening during that trip.

The following few days went by and Gabby got more movement back. John took them to the hospital for a check-up and to get the wound checked.

She also had to check in at the physio department. She was okay with this as she went to the spinal unit every week practising, so she was more than happy to go and see what she was capable of now. She went in there wondering how she would do. She asked if they had callipers. John told her they wanted to see if she could stand. She looked at him and wasn't sure if he was joking, but he was being deadly serious. She asked if she could try with the callipers first to see how it feels so she knew she could do that already.

He said, 'Okay, that will work.'

They fitted her up with some callipers. They didn't feel the same as the ones she was used to but she tried them out and stood up inside the bars. She stood up and instead of the normal movement, she found that she could move her legs like she could before she was injured. They were all watching and after she had done a few walks up and down with the callipers, John asked her if she would try taking them off and just see if she could stand.

She had a physio either side of her to make sure she didn't crumple into a heap on the floor. She agreed, so the two physios took her hands and helped her stand. When they asked her how she felt, she just stood there. With no callipers, and no rails. She didn't want to say a thing.

She just heard one voice, Lloyd, saying, 'Mummy, you're doing it.'

She cried, huge happy tears pouring down her face, and that set off Lloyd and Carl and then Isabelle too was sobbing. They were all so happy.

She sat down and they asked if she wanted to try standing with just one physio. She said she'd try and he took her hand. She stood up. She felt nervous and a bit like she was glued to the spot, not daring to move in case she fell. But her legs were standing firm. No sign of her falling.
She sat back down and John said he thought they should stop for the day now, she'd done a lot and they didn't want to overdo things. She was glad as the emotion of it along with the walking with the callipers and the standing was actually more tiring than she thought.
They checked how her back was healing and it was lovely and clean, and she went out in her chair back to the car. Everyone was asking her how it felt, if she remembered what it was like and if she thought it was going to keep getting better. She suddenly felt upset and wasn't sure what was going on. She should be really happy; she had so much to be grateful for.
She didn't know why she was feeling sad. She sat in the car wondering what was going on in her head. So, she sat quietly and let everyone else chat on the way back to the house.

When they got back, she said, 'I think I need to spend a few minutes alone if nobody minds.'
They all said, 'Not at all,' and Carl checked if she was okay.
She said. 'Yes, fine. I just need a few minutes.'

She went in the bedroom and closed the door and sat on the bed. She realised she hadn't been taking the time to talk to her angels and she had not been doing her meditations either. She realised she was sad because at such a great occasion she should have been thanking the angels for being there for her and helping her get this far. She spoke to the angels that afternoon. She wanted to tell them everything that had been happening. She thanked them belatedly for everything they had helped her with. She asked them to be with her each day through her life. She did a meditation and dug out her journals and did some writing.
After she had done all this, she felt a lot better. She felt much calmer and knew she had done the right thing. She had been sad because she'd left what is to her, her best friend, out of such a momentous moment. She felt guilty. She now had thanked her angels and all was well. She knew from then she wouldn't ever forget to keep talking to them.

CHAPTER 75

They spent the rest of the trip going to water parks and to see baseball games. They were soon hooked on the Tampa Bay Rays. They even managed to meet up with their friends, Christine and David. It was great to introduce them to Isabelle and John and fill them in with all that had been happening for them.

Gabby hadn't been posting things on her social network because she didn't want to have her mum hear things second-hand, so she kept quiet and just posted a few pictures. She showed Christine how she could move her legs and how things had changed.

In the days that had come by, she found she now had her control of her bladder and bowels. That was something that was almost better than the walking. It was like a dream; she kept thinking she'd wake up any moment.

At the end of the baseball game, she made a comment to David, 'I bet I could walk across that field now. I've been practising.'

David was very competitive and a very positive person. He had contacts, and before they left he said, 'Come this way.'

They all followed and he said to Gabby, 'Want to take a walk?'
She looked at John and he said, 'You can try.'
Carl got his phone out to take a video, David took her hand and she carefully stood up. She took a step, and then another, Lloyd walked closely behind with his mum's chair in case she needed to sit down. She very slowly walked all the way across the baseball field. When they reached the end, everyone cheered. David swung her round and then helped her back in her chair with Lloyd's help. Carl had it all on video and they were all so happy.
Christine had said many years before that she was glad God had brought them together but for them to be a part of this special time was something none of them would ever forget. And for John, this was amazing progress. He told her to now take things easy for the rest of the trip. Stand and take a few steps but don't go mad too soon. She took his advice and was careful.
She made sure she kept up with her spiritual connection. She knew this was something special. This opportunity had come after so many years of bad things. Then changing the way she looked at life had literally changed her own life. She was looking forward to going back to the spinal unit and showing all those patients what can be achieved.

Bad things happen to good people sometimes to teach them when something good happens to really grab hold of it and fully appreciate it. Be thankful and never forget who helped along the way.

Before they knew it, they were back on the private plane, flying back to London and then onward to the Island. They had lots of hugs and lots of tears. Gabby had nearly finished proofreading Isabelle's book but Isabelle said there was some more to come and she gave Gabby a wink. Then she knew that they were all going to appear in her life story now.

Going back to the Island was a big shock to the system and they all felt sad, especially Lloyd, who was going to miss Milo. But they were going to play Fortnite together and could message each other too. Isabelle and John said they would visit them next time, so that would be something special to look forward to.

They slept well on the plane and the short journey back to the Island was nice and smooth. When they got back to the house, Carl's parents, Freda and Les, were there as they had been feeding their cat. Carl and Lloyd looked at Gabby and they all did a silent nod. His parents had no idea what they had been doing on their trip, so they all went in the house and Gabby had bought them gifts from the little tourist shop in Clearwater.

They sat down and as they did so, Gabby stood up and walked two steps towards them. Freda stood up and grabbed her for a hug and Les started to cry. It was an emotional moment. That evening, Gabby wanted to speak to her own mum and let her know how they all were, so they did a video chat and Lloyd held the phone and said, 'Mummy wants to show you something.' Gabby did the same; she stood up and took two steps, and said, 'Surprise.' Yvette burst into tears – huge tears running down her face. She couldn't take it in. She said she'd have to sit down and Gabby sat down too. Gabby sat and told her what they had been doing and said they hadn't told anyone in case it didn't work and they would be disappointed. This was something Yvette thought she'd never see again. She was so unbelievably happy.

CHAPTER 76

The next few days were taken up with washing the holiday clothes and getting back into the swing of normal life again. Gabby's proofreading was keeping her very busy and she was making enough money from it to not have to do anything else. This worked well around the things Lloyd wanted to do. This also meant she could pop over and see her mum more often and make sure she was doing okay.

She went the following week to the spinal unit as she hadn't been in a few weeks. This time though she wouldn't be using callipers in the physio. She went to her room as usual when she arrived and threw her stuff on her bed. She kept using her chair, but she made the most of walking too. She was conscious of how much she did in case she overdid things.

As normal, she went into the cafe to get a drink and contact Carl and Lloyd to let them know she had arrived safely. She then she logged on to her laptop to check for work coming in whilst drinking her coffee.

As she was sitting there, a pretty young girl walked over to her and said, 'Hi Gabby.'

Gabby looked at her and thought she recognised her but couldn't think who she was, then realised it was Rose. She looked amazing; she was walking really well and she looked like a happy, confident young lady again.

Gabby said she was so pleased for her.

Rose said she'd just come in for a check-up and she was allowed home now. She'd be back to college soon and she wanted to do art and continue working towards her hairdressing.

Gabby said she thought that would be amazing.

Rose gave her a hug and said, 'If it wasn't for our chat, I don't think I'd be here now. Thank you so much.'

She then turned and walked away. Gabby knew at that moment, that was the reason. The reason she had to go through so much was to save not just herself, but also to save Rose.

Our lives are mapped out for us all and whatever happens within it is what is meant to happen, the good and the bad. We attract what we put out into the universe. This can be consciously by focusing on manifesting something you want but it can also be an unconscious manifestation. This is the Law of Attraction.

So, was Gabby's life so far a terrible bundle of accidents or was it Gabby unconsciously manifesting these things into her life? And had the law of attraction taken effect after learning a new way of doing things and always remembering to be grateful?

We all have a purpose in life. Some of us go through life not finding that purpose and some find things the hard way. Gabby found her purpose. She was meant to experience all these things so that when it came to it she was able to help someone and to help that person to keep going and to show her to never give up on her precious time on this earth. She found that purpose through the law of attraction.

About the Author

I live in Jersey in the Channel Islands with my husband Steve and our son Milo and cat Pixar. It's a small island, close to France. I wrote this book after growing up reading horsey books and thought this would have a different edge to it.

There are many people who have spinal injuries and you never hear of them in fictional books. This is something I wanted to change. So here it is and I hope you like it.

I am always on the lookout for a cure for spinal cord injuries and hope this book will go some way to get some more awareness out there to what you have to live with when you suffer one of these horrific injuries.

35369162R00176

Printed in Poland
by Amazon Fulfillment
Poland Sp. z o.o., Wrocław